Together at Last

Together at Last

SUMANA ROY CHOWDHURY

Srishti
PUBLISHERS & DISTRIBUTORS

Srishti Publishers & Distributors
A unit of AJR Publishing LLP
212A, Peacock Lane
Shahpur Jat, New Delhi – 110 049
editorial@srishtipublishers.com

First published by
Srishti Publishers & Distributors in 2021

10 9 8 7 6 5 4 3 2 1

This is a work of fiction. The characters, places, organizations and events described in this book are either a work of the author's imagination or have been used fictitiously. Any resemblance to people, living or dead, places, events, communities or organizations is purely coincidental.

Prologue

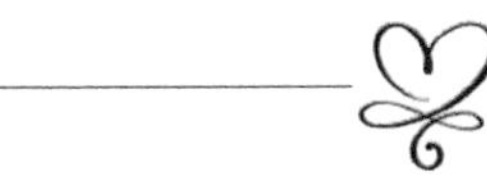

Present day
Burdwan

It was his eighty-first birthday, although he did not remember it.

Jatin cracked open his eyes and gazed at the plaster that was peeling off the high ceiling in his bedroom. For a while he lay perfectly still, preferring to spend a few more moments in the zone between sleep and wakefulness. He knew that another day stretched ahead of him and his tired mind expected this one to be no different from the innumerable others that had preceded it. But a nagging feeling at the corner of his mind told him that there was something special today; something that he ought to remember. He racked his brain and then gave up, assuming that whatever it was, it would come back to him in due time. It always did. He stretched his arms above his head, to feel an immediate pain assault his creaking bones.

And just as he was about to raise his body from the bed, a familiar voice addressed him, “Good morning! Wake up, lazy bones!”

He looked around the room, startled. For years now, Jatin had been living alone and he did not expect to have any visitors so early in the morning. As he scanned the room, his eyes came to rest on a dusky young girl, dressed in a cotton salwar-kameez, with curly locks of hair and an oval face. She stood at the foot of his bed and gazed at him adoringly with her wide brown eyes. Jatin sighed with relief; it was only his eighteen-year-old neighbour. She was one of the very few people who still visited him, but of late Jatin had noticed that the frequency of her visits had increased.

"You scared me. Why are you here again?" he exclaimed, feigning irritation although inwardly he was glad to see the girl, as always.

She ignored the reprimand and came to sit next to him on the high bed with her feet dangling well above the floor.

"Happy birthday! What are your plans for the day?"

Ah! So that's what it was, thought Jatin to himself. *Today's my birthday!*

Aloud he said to the girl, "Plans? Do you know how old I am today?"

She shrugged and he answered his rhetorical question, "Eighty-one! I am eighty-one years old."

Even as he spoke, Jatin wondered where all the time had gone. His mind wandered back to his splendid childhood days and to the birthday parties that his mother used to organize for him. Back then, birthdays meant excitement and cakes and presents and celebrations. It meant being surrounded by people who loved and cared for him; people who were now all long gone. He had noticed that in his thoughts; the days of his childhood always seemed to be more colourful and full of hope than they had appeared to him then.

"It's strange how time changes everything," he said aloud to the eager girl who sat watching him. "When I was young, I used to look forward to my birthday for the whole year. And now, no one even remembers it, including me."

His young and energetic neighbour clicked her tongue and cast him an exasperated look.

"Come on now, get up! This won't do. I am here to wish you on your birthday, am I not? And that's because I love you and care for you. Get up and get ready, then we can go out somewhere. We can go to the park and have ice-cream like we usually do…or perhaps—" She was tugging at his hand, trying to force him to stand up.

"Alright, alright!" Jatin replied, holding up his hand to fend off the girl. "We'll go later. Go home now and come back later. We'll see what we can do then."

Jatin pretended to not notice the slight tremor in his hand as he held it up to the girl. This had been happening for a few months now and he had been worried when the tremors had first started, but by now, he had gotten used to them. He had been putting off the thought of going to see a doctor for the past six months.

"Okay! I'll go away for now," said the girl, looking dejected at Jatin's lack of enthusiasm at her plans for his birthday. "In any case, Anupama will be here any moment to clean the house and I don't like her one bit."

Before Jatin had an opportunity to look up, the girl was gone. He raised himself from the bed and shuffled towards the bedroom window, pulling aside the curtains. Blinking at the harsh sunlight in his face, he looked at the chaotic high street in front of his house. People of all ages seemed to be in a mad rush to reach their respective destinations. Cars honked in frustration as they tried to swerve their way out of the ugly morning traffic congestion, young mothers frantically ran with their kids in tow, in order to reach the school bus that waited impatiently. He sighed. The world as he had known it no longer existed and Jatin's mind once again travelled back to his youth. Back in the day, Burdwan used to be an idyllic countryside with lush green fields which had extended for miles before their house.

The sound of the doorbell caused Jatin to come back to the present and he walked as quickly as he could to open the door for Anupama, his house help. She gave him an irritated look as she brushed past him into the house. As he closed the door, he noticed that the once-magnificent front door made of mahogany wood was now covered with cracks and cobwebs and that the intricately carved designs on it were now worn away, replaced by an almost flat surface. He still remembered how his father had spent days deciding on the front door that was to be chosen for the brand new house that had been built years ago.

"I have been ringing the doorbell for ten minutes," grumbled Anupama from the kitchen. "Why can't you open the door sooner? You do not realize that I have lots of other things to do as well. If you don't open the door on time from tomorrow onwards, then I will not wait for you."

Jatin snapped at the woman.

"Stop complaining, Anupama. I will open the door on time and you will not have to wait."

He heard her mutter something under her breath as she walked back into the living room with the broom in her hand.

"What's that you say?" he asked sharply and the woman shook her head, realizing that she had gone too far. He watched her as she started to sweep the dust off the floor.

Ten minutes later, when Jatin came out of the bathroom after brushing his teeth, he found Anupama busy speaking with someone on her phone, with the broom lying in the exact position where it had been when he had gone into the bathroom. Upon seeing him, she quickly retreated into the kitchen and brought him his customary cup of morning tea.

"Here, have your tea," she said, placing the cup and saucer on the old wooden dining table that stood in the corner of the living room.

Jatin's right hand trembled as he raised the cup to his lips. He steadied it with his left and sipped upon his tea, grimacing at the excessive sweetness of the mild liquid. He eyed Anupama thoughtfully who had resumed sweeping the floor. Although he had employed her, he was scared of her sharp tongue and contemplated on whether he should tell her what was on his mind or not. Finally mustering up some courage, he cleared his throat.

"Anupama…"

"Yes?"

"The bathroom is very dirty. It is so slippery that I almost fell down last night. You will have to clean it."

She cast him a look that made Jatin turn his gaze back to his tea cup again.

Encouraged by this minor victory, Anupama began another tirade, "Dadu, this is exactly why no one wants to work in this house. I had cleaned the bathroom only two days ago and now you say that it is dirty again? I have to clean your house and cook for you. In addition, you expect me to clean your bathroom every day."

Jatin clicked his tongue impatiently.

"Do you know that this house is almost as old as I am?" he asked the woman who stood looking at him with an expression of disbelief on her face. "My father had built it with lots of care – brick by brick."

Noticing the look on her face, Jatin quickly continued, "I have a point. What I mean to say is that this is my ancestral house and you keep it so dirty, Anupama. If I had any strength left in me, then I would have cleaned it myself."

Anupama was about to open her mouth to reply, but then closed it again.

"Okay, okay. I will clean the bathroom," she said in a conciliatory tone, offering Jatin her hand as he attempted to get up from the dining table after putting down the half full cup of tea.

"The tea tastes horrible. Where did you learn to make such tea?" he asked her as he grasped her hand and walked towards the balcony outside the living room. He noticed with some satisfaction that she did not answer back to that statement.

Although Jatin was often exasperated with Anupama, the two of them were fond of each other as well. She had been working for him for almost ten years now. Ever since his health had begun to deteriorate after the stroke that he had suffered two years ago, she had been looking after him well. The stroke had partially incapacitated Jatin, making it impossible for him to continue with the steady medical practice that he had been able to set up in Burdwan over the years. His had been one of the first clinics that Burdwan had seen, although with time, many more such clinics had popped up all over town, with younger doctors who were trained in modern medicine also setting up their shops. However, over the years, Jatin had earned the reputation of being a dependable doctor and he had a very loyal base of patients who used to visit his clinic frequently till he used to practice.

The stroke had also made it difficult for Jatin to go out for chores like before, and it was now left to Anupama to take care of most things for him. She cooked and cleaned for him, although not very well, and also brought him his groceries and medicines. In return, Jatin paid her a good salary and also supported her son's education.

"*Achcha*, Dadu?" she started conversationally, as they reached the balcony that was bathed in the morning sunlight, just the way Jatin liked it.

"Yes?"

"Don't you have anyone in your family?"

Jatin was silent for a moment.

This is what he disliked about Anupama. The woman just could not mind her own business!

"No," he replied shortly, keeping his opinions about her to himself.

"Oh!" she replied, probably deciding that it would be a better idea to not probe further and changed tracks.

"Dadu, have you seen a doctor lately? The tremors in your hand have been increasing."

"I am fine," he replied, as Anupama helped him into his favourite armchair and handed him the newspaper. "Can you go and complete your work Anupama, and leave me in peace for a while?"

"Alright. Here, read the newspaper, while I complete my chores," said the woman, deciding to heed his words for a change.

Jatin settled into the armchair and turned his attention to the first page of the newspaper to immediately fling it down in his lap.

"These days the newspapers, only have no ethics left," he said aloud, to no one in particular. "Everything is 'breaking news'. News has to be sensationalized to make it more entertaining, so that the publications can sell their newspapers!"

The sun had risen well above the horizon when Jatin felt someone shake him awake. He opened his eyes to see Anupama gaze down at him.

"Wake up, Dadu! It's past eleven o'clock and you fell asleep again. Then you complain that you cannot sleep at night. Get up now! I have cleaned the bathroom and have filled warm water in the bucket for your bath. Go on, take a bath and then have your meal. I have kept it covered on the dining table."

He looked at the woman blankly for a few moments, trying to place her and his surroundings. Then he grasped Anupama's hand to rise from the chair as his senses returned after the temporary bout of amnesia.

"You should get a full-time ayah to look after you, you know, Dadu," offered Anupama. "I cannot be here to look after you for the whole day, and you…"

"Have I asked you to look after me the whole day?" Jatin snapped at her, causing Anupama to go quiet.

"Alright, I am leaving then!" she said, heading towards the front door with Jatin following her. "If you need something, then you can call me on my phone. Remember to keep the phone hung around your neck or else you will forget where it is, like the other day…and will not be able to contact me. Also, shut and bolt the door properly. The things that happen in this city these days are unbelievable. Only the other day there was news that an old couple was murdered…"

Jatin had zoned her chatter out and was about to close the door when he saw his young neighbour outside the front door again.

"Come on, let's go out! You said in the morning that you would," she said brightly.

"No, no. Go away now!" said Jatin firmly, and saw her face fall. He ignored it. He was in no mood to go out.

Anupama, who was out of the door by then stopped her monologue for a moment and glared at Jatin.

"What? I am going. Can't you see that? Why would I hang around here after I have completed my work?"

Jatin shook his head and shut and bolted the door on the two mad women outside and let out a sigh of relief.

By the time Jatin completed his morning chores and finished lunch, it was 12.30 p.m. This was the time of the day that he dreaded the most. There were at least eight more hours of the day to fill and he had nothing to do. He switched on the old television set in the living room and flipped through the channels to see what was on. A *saas-bahu* serial. A slapstick comedy movie. Then news about wars and people dying and suffering. Everything on the television seemed to have been tailored to satisfy the voyeuristic appetite of a world that had gone grossly wrong since his wondrous childhood days. He flipped the switch to shut out the harsh world that grated on his senses and dozed off.

One

1958, Burdwan
Jatin's house

The doorbell rang. Jatin ran over to open the heavy mahogany front door that was carved intricately with floral designs. The house was newly-built by his father and the design of the front door had been a topic of several hot debates in the Majumdar household before a consensus had been reached about its design.

He opened the door to find his neighbour Aditi outside. She was dressed in her usual cotton salwar-kameez with her curly hair dishevelled, causing a few locks to fall over her forehead. Her big brown eyes were twinkling and full of life. He ran his sharp brown eyes over her, taking in her appearance and noticed her do the same; her eyes lighting up at what she saw. Jatin was all of eighteen that year, with a mop of black curly hair, and a lean physique. At five feet ten inches of height, he towered above her modest five feet two inches.

"Come on Jatin!" she said. "Let's go out. You had promised me yesterday that you would go out with me today!"

He glanced behind him cautiously and put a finger to his lips to silence Aditi.

"Sshhhh. Not so loud. She will hear you," he whispered to her.

Aditi covered her mouth with her palm to suppress a giggle. As Jatin had predicted, a voice came from within the house.

"Who is it, Jatin? Is it that Aditi again? I must tell her mother about this. Back in our day, we could never imagine running around town like that girl does. In those days, girls would stay at home and…"

Mrs Majumdar emerged grumbling from inside and cut her complaints short when she spotted her young guest at the door.

"What is it, Aditi?" asked the short plump woman as she sternly peered at the girl over the rim of her gold-framed glasses. Jatin thought to himself that any girl of a lesser disposition would have been scared to speak further at such a look; but not his Aditi.

"*Namashkar, Mashima,*" replied Aditi, demurely joining her palms in a namaste, immediately causing the older woman to soften her stance. She had known Aditi since she had been a little girl. Truth be told, Mrs Majumdar was in fact quite fond of her, but she disliked her impulsive nature and felt it necessary to keep the girl in check.

"Namashkar, namashkar," she said dismissively. "What are you doing here at eleven in the morning? Don't you have any work to do at home?"

"I wanted to ask Jatin if we could go out today," replied Aditi boldly, ignoring Jatin's desperate gestures.

"No, not now Aditi," replied Mrs Majumdar sternly. "Jatin has some chores to do. I want him to get me groceries from the market."

"I'll go with him," came the immediate response, causing Jatin to smile at her lovingly and Mrs Majumdar to shake her head in frustration.

"Alright then. There's no arguing with young people these days, is there? Why would you worry about what people have to say about the two of you roaming all around the countryside together the whole day? In our days, my father would have a heart attack if he knew that I was running around town with a boy. Anyway, I know when I am beaten. Jatin, come inside and get the grocery list and bag from me."

Jatin meekly followed her inside while throwing Aditi a backward glance and gesturing for her to wait.

They walked to the grocer's shop together, an achingly young couple, with a spring in their step and the whole world seemingly at their feet. On the way back, they meandered around the small town. They went in to the only park in their town, which was deserted in the middle of the hot summer day. They sat on a bench in a secluded corner of the park and Jatin watched on indulgently as Aditi licked at the ice-cream cone that he had bought for her. He reached out his thumb to wipe off the white moustache that the ice-cream had made on her upper lip. The journey from being childhood friends to lovers had been organic for them and neither of them had ever thought of the possibility of being with anyone else.

"Umm. Let go of me, Jatin," said Aditi as he pulled her towards him once she had eaten the last of the cone.

"Why?"

"What if someone sees us?"

Jatin looked around him at the empty park.

"Who is here to see us?" he questioned, pulling her close once more. "Stop making excuses. Stay here and stay still…"

She obediently settled her head on his shoulder and mumbled. "There are people around. Didn't you hear what Mashima said today? That people are talking about us."

"Since when did you start worrying about what people say?"

She hesitated and then said, "Well, not exactly about people, but what if my Ma asked me about what I am doing with you? What should I tell her, Jatin? You know how my parents are and what they think about…"

She trailed off leaving the incomplete sentence dangling in the air between them. Jatin lowered his head to look into the small face that he adored.

"Tell her that you are with your husband-to-be."

"*Dhyat!*"

"What? Won't you marry me?" he asked tickling her waist and causing her to squeal.

"Tell me? Won't you?"

"No, I won't," she replied with a mischievous grin. "I cannot get married to you just because you have bought me an ice-cream cone."

"Well then. Tell me what else would you like me to get you?" asked Jatin letting go of her, his expression turning serious.

"Hey, I was only joking," she said appeasingly, noticing his change of mood.

Jatin was silent. Even though in jest, Aditi had touched a raw nerve.

"I don't like such jokes, Aditi. Just tell me, what more can I get you?"

"I don't need anything as long as I have you Jatin," she replied cuddling up to him.

Her response appeased him to an extent, but his mind had now travelled elsewhere. He looked at his feet. Aditi turned his face towards her, trying to gain back his attention.

"What are you thinking about?" she asked. "I have you and you have me, Jatin. What more do we need?"

Jatin gave her a strange look, and for a fleeting moment, he clearly saw how different they were as people.

"I need lots more, Aditi," he said slowly. "I want to go out and explore the world, I want to experience life... all of it; the good, the bad and the ugly. I want to study medicine so that I can be a doctor and heal people, and no one will have to die again without proper treatment."

He paused and their eyes met. They both knew what had remained unsaid and Aditi promptly changed the subject to lighten the mood.

"What do you mean by saying that you want to travel the whole world? You mean Calcutta, don't you?"

"Calcutta, Bombay, England…"

"England? Isn't there an ocean in between? No, no! I am scared of water and I don't even know how to swim."

"Well," replied Jatin gravely, a small smile returning to his face, "You won't have to swim to London. I will take you there on a ship or even an airplane."

"An airplane?" she asked, her eyes growing wider. "No Jatin, I am scared of heights. I cannot even go and stand on the roof of our two-storied house. Whenever I look down from there, I feel scared that I will fall down. I get nightmares where I dream that I have fallen off the roof and I see that I am lying on the ground in a pool of blood. You know how scared I am of blood, don't you?"

Jatin hugged her. Although he didn't say it aloud but he admitted to himself that he would be scared to get on to an airplane too. A ship to London seemed like a safer option.

"Okay then. I will go and explore the world, while you can stay back in Burdwan," he said to her, trying to reduce her anxiety.

"And what will I do when you are out exploring the world?" she asked, unaware of how vulnerable she sounded. "The only world that I know of is you and this town."

For the first time, Jatin realised the impact of his decisions on Aditi and her life. So far, he had only thought about his own dreams and had assumed that all other parts of his life would somehow come together, so he had been unprepared for her question.

"You are home to me, Aditi," he replied after a pause. "When everything is done, then I will always return to you and I know that I will find you waiting for me when I come back…"

She looked doubtful and he placed a finger under her chin to raise her face towards him to kiss her.

Two

The sweltering heat had made it impossible to stay indoors on the hot summer evening in June. Jatin sat sprawled on an armchair in the balcony outside the living room of their house, with a book in his hands. He wiped off the beads of sweat that had formed on his forehead with the back of his hand for what seemed to be the hundredth time and tried to focus on the book once more. The sound of a passing car made him look up at the mud road outside the house. He recognised the cream-coloured Ambassador immediately and followed its progress with his eyes until it turned into the driveway in the house next to theirs and disappeared from sight. Cars were a luxury that only a chosen few in Burdwan could afford to own; with most people preferring to use rickshaws and bicycles for their conveyance around town. Aditi's family happened to be one of the few fortunate ones who were wealthy enough to own a car. Her father, Mr Sanyal, was a judge at the local courtroom and an influential figure in town.

Jatin was about to return to his book when his attention was diverted yet again by voices that he heard from the living room behind him. He peered through the crack in the balcony door to see his father enter the room, followed by two men, whom Jatin recognised as farmers from the neighbouring village. The maid followed the men and placed a cup of tea along with an evening snack on the centre table.

Jatin watched his father settle down on the sofa behind the table and take a sip of tea while the men stood in front of him with folded hands, waiting for the maid to leave. Once she was out of earshot, one of them spoke up, "Majumdar sahib, please help us sir. The land is all we have and if we lose that too, then our families will starve to death…"

Mr Majumdar took a bite of the warm samosa from the plate before him and chewed on it as the men looked on anxiously.

"You see, I am a lawyer," he said finally, wiping the crumbs off his thick moustache, "and I can help you get your land back. But for that you will have to go to the court and register your case."

Mr Majumdar paused at this point and looked at the dejected faces that stared back at him blankly.

"But sahib, we are not educated and don't know what to do…"

Jatin's father held up his hand. "I will help you with the process. That is not the problem here…"

He left the unfinished sentence hanging in the air and the men caught on quickly.

"Sahib, we are poor and we don't have any money. That's why we have come to you to ask for your help. Registering a case in the court will be expensive and we wanted to request you to excuse the fees."

Mr Majumdar's expression changed and he fixed the two men with a hard stare, making them squirm.

"You must understand that I do not run a charity organisation. I am a lawyer and I have a fee which you will have to pay. So go home, think about how you can pay me and come back tomorrow if you have the answer. Then we can decide on how we plan the case to get your land back."

The men exchanged uncertain looks. They bowed to Mr Majumdar, knowing that they had been dismissed and shuffled out of the room. Jatin was unaware that he had been clenching his fists while he witnessed the scene unfold before him. He could empathise with the two men who had come to beg his father for help. He had memories of the early years of his life when the family had lived in a small one-bedroom house and had slept most nights on a half-empty stomach. This was the time when Mr Majumdar's practice in law wasn't yet as successful as it was today. Jatin remembered how his mother would struggle hard to make ends meet while his father left the running of the household, on his meagre income, completely to her. The heated arguments between his parents still rang in his ears.

"We have to pay Jatin's school fees," his mother would say. "I need money for that. Whatever you earn, Jahar, you spend it on your books or on cigarettes."

"I work hard all day and when I come home, you begin to nag me," grumbled her husband. "Can I not get a moment of peace?"

His voice was raised. Jatin saw his mother flinch but she still didn't back down.

"The boy is in his growing years and needs nutritious food. If we continue in this way, then soon we won't be able to afford even meals..."

"Will you shut up, Sunita?" yelled his father. "Why do I allow you to live in my house if you cannot help with anything? I bring in the money and the least that you can do to help is to see how to use it well. So stop nagging me. I am hungry, get me something to eat."

Jatin had watched from the corner of the room as his father turned his back to his wife, immersing himself in one of his thick books on law, indicating that the conversation was over. The boy saw his mother's eyes fill with tears as she headed to the kitchen to get her husband his evening meal. He knew that like most other nights, his mother would go hungry that night as well. He hated those books that his father loved so much and he wished that he could burn each one of them.

"Jatin? *Jatin?*"

He returned to the present as he heard his father call out to him and entered the living room through the balcony door.

"Come and sit here with me," said Mr Majumdar patting the sofa beside him as his son appeared before him.

Jatin obliged and glanced at his father sideways, noticing the unforgiving sun's rays highlight the wrinkles on the man's face, the strands of grey in his hair and the fast-receding hairline. They sat in an awkward silence as neither of them knew what to say to the other and Jatin watched his father drain the last of his tea. Mr Majumdar cleared his throat and began.

"Your summer holidays will be over soon and you need to decide what you want to do next, Jatin. You have completed school and I know that your grades are good. With those, you should be able to get admission to a good college in Calcutta. We can look at some of the law schools."

Jatin had already decided what he wanted to do with his life and he resented that his father insisted on making decisions on his behalf.

"I don't want to be a lawyer," he replied firmly, turning up his chin as he spoke. "You know that I want to study medicine, Baba."

Mr Majumdar studied his son with a hard stare which made Jatin shift in the sofa uncomfortably.

"Jatin, you are my only son and I have many plans for your life," he said after a pause. "Why do you want to make your life difficult? Study law and come back here to practice. You are getting everything on a platter. I have slogged hard all my life to earn all of this and now you are in a position to enjoy the fruits of my hard work. I want you to study law and carry on my legacy."

Jatin drew in his breath sharply. It frustrated him that his father had never made an attempt to understand him. He did not want to return to Burdwan or to carry on his father's legacy. In Jatin's mind, the hardships that the family had endured during his early years and the profession of law were intertwined and he never wanted to revisit those days again.

"Baba, your legacy is yours. I want to make my life on my own," he averted his eyes from his father's stern gaze and added, "...also, you know that I will never return to Burdwan once I leave."

His father sighed.

"Jatin, when I had built this house, I had built it with you in mind. You are my only son and after you complete your education, I want you to come back and live here."

Jatin had seen his father stand for hours in the blazing sun for months on end as the man had watched this house being built. He understood that the house was more than brick and mortar to his father and that, in a way, it was a symbol of his eventual success. But the house had always suffocated Jatin, although it was large and airy; and he yearned to get away from it.

"The house is yours, Baba and I have told you before that I will never live here," he said resolutely, watching with satisfaction the flicker of emotion on his father's usually expressionless face.

Encouraged at being able to evoke a reaction, he continued, "I want to study medicine and be a doctor. Over the summer holidays, I have spent lots of time in the library and have listed all the good medical colleges in Calcutta. I have also sent out applications to the colleges that I have short-listed and am waiting for their response."

His father's mouth dropped open.

"Be reasonable, Jatin. You know nothing about the medical schools in Calcutta."

Jatin said nothing and Mr Majumdar's face clouded at his son's impertinence.

"Jatin, I know that we have had such discussions before and I let it go at that time, taking it to be your immaturity. But this is your life that we are talking about and I will not allow you to make flippant decisions. I want you to stop this nonsense about medical school. I have spoken with some friends of mine and have already made arrangements for you to study law in Calcutta."

"Baba, I have made my decision," said Jatin, looking his father in the eye. "I want to be a doctor."

There was a tense silence as the two men sat looking at each other, caught in a deadlock, with the metallic clicking of the fan overhead being the only sound in the room

"Well, in that case Jatin…" said Mr Majumdar after several moments, "...I cannot fund your education. Medicine is an uncertain profession and Calcutta is an expensive city. I do not want to waste my hard-earned money on your whims."

The predictable response made it impossible for Jatin to resist the urge to laugh out aloud. All through his childhood he had seen his father hold money as a ransom over his and his mother's head, to make them do things that they did not want to. But this time, he was prepared.

"I don't need your money," Jatin shot back. "I have applied for the national scholarship and given my grades, I know that I will receive it. If I receive the scholarship, then I will also get a stipend to bear my expenses in the city. I had told you about the application when I had sent it out, but you were, as usual, too busy with yourself to pay any attention to me and my life. But yes, I do not expect you to support me... financially."

He added the last word for effect and saw that it had not been lost on his father. Jatin was well-versed with Mr Majumdar's ego, having inherited it himself, and now he braced himself for what he knew was coming.

"Well, I cannot stop you from doing what you have already decided upon," said Mr Majumdar, in an icy-cold voice, "but I want you to be aware of the fact that Calcutta is a ruthless city and that medicine is a tough profession. I do not doubt that you will be able to get into a good college with your grades, but I will be very surprised if you can successfully complete your course there, given your immaturity. You are not made of the material that is needed to make one successful in such a world and you will see that you will have to come back to me soon. But till that day arrives, I will not stop you. Go ahead and see if you can prove me wrong."

The words had been intended to hurt and they had achieved their objective. Jatin jumped up.

"I did not expect your encouragement, Baba, and I did not get it. I will let you know when I am ready to leave your house."

With that he turned and stormed out of the room, banging the door behind him as he left.

Three

Jatin was sitting at the study table in his room, reading the brochure that he had received from Nilratan Medical College the previous day. Along with the brochure had come in an admission letter as well as a letter with an offer for a national scholarship to the college of his choice. Jatin was so engrossed in the documents that he did not notice Aditi walk into the room, until she peered over his shoulder and asked, "What's that, Jatin?"

"Nothing," he replied, startled, turning the booklet face-down on an impulse.

She stood with her hands on her hips and fixed him with a suspicious look in her eyes.

"What are you hiding? Let me have a look at that..."

She attempted to snatch the booklet out of his hands, but Jatin was faster. He caught her by the arms and pulled her into his lap, clasping her hands in his.

"Stop it, Aditi! Sit still. I have something to tell you."

A shade of consternation came over her transparent features.

"Why do you hide everything from me?" she asked, puffing out her cheeks. Jatin suppressed a smile and held out the admission letter to her.

"Ok. Here it is. Read it."

She snatched it from his hand and ran her eyes over the offer letter, then turned towards him with her eyes twinkling.

"You got into medical college? And you got a scholarship?" she hugged him tightly. "I am so happy. You idiot! Why didn't you tell me that you had applied?"

He smiled at her reaction and held her close. Aditi was the first person with whom he had shared this news and her reaction had been just as he had anticipated. But Jatin knew that in her initial excitement, she had missed out on an important detail.

"Aditi…" he said carefully, "...take another look at the letter."

She raised her head from his chest and took the letter from him once more, knitting her brows together as she studied it closely.

"First of July?" she said looking up at him. "But that's only ten days away, Jatin!"

He watched several conflicting expressions cross her face, none of which he could latch on to.

"Aditi," he said softly, "you always knew that I would have to leave someday."

"Someday," she said, "but I did not know that the cursed day would come so soon."

She was biting her lower lip, like she did when she was agitated and Jatin could sense her inner turmoil.

"Aditi… look at me!"

She did and he saw that her eyes were moist. A familiar feeling of guilt settled in the pit of his stomach.

"Both of us knew that this moment was inevitable. I have to leave Burdwan," he said, searching for the right words as he spoke.

"Nothing about my life is hidden from you, Aditi and you know that I cannot continue to live here. You know that every single day here suffocates me. I applied for the national scholarship because I don't want to depend on my father. I know him too well and he refused to fund my education if I did not agree to study law. I do not want to live my life by that man's whims anymore. I want to be free."

Jatin had never been good with words and although he fumbled initially, as he continued to speak, his words gained momentum.

"I don't want to be Baba's puppet all my life, like Ma. Everything has always been about him – his life, his ambitions and I never fit anywhere in it."

Jatin's breath came in spurts as it did when he was agitated and Aditi held a finger to his lips to silence him.

"Ssshhh Jatin. Don't say anything more. I can understand."

That's all that he had needed to hear at that moment and he hugged her close. She somehow always knew the right thing to say. She always knew how to make him feel better.

"When will you be back?" she asked, her face still buried in his shoulder.

He was silent as the guilt in his heart grew heavier. He could feel the warm wetness of her tears on his shoulder and he clenched his jaws. At that moment, Jatin felt like the most selfish person on the planet.

"I don't know," he murmured truthfully and then added, "please understand that I am not leaving you, Aditi. I am leaving this town."

He felt her body stiffen and pulled back to look at her tear-streaked face. He placed his lips on hers to stop further conversation. She kissed him back, locking her arms around his neck and allowing him to run his fingers through the wild locks of her hair which had come loose. He felt her shiver as he slipped his hand under her kurta and ran his fingers over the smooth skin on her stomach which was in sharp contrast to the rough fabric of her attire.

Ten days flew by faster than they should have and soon the day of Jatin's departure had arrived.

Aditi stood at the corner of his bedroom where three suitcases lay on the bed in various stages of disarray. Mrs Majumdar fussed about the room, making several journeys from the cupboard to the bed and back again, while the keys tied to the *pallu* of her saree jingled loudly.

"Let me help, Mashima," offered Aditi. The huge wooden clock that hung on the wall of the room above Jatin's bed showed 4 p.m. Time seemed to gallop ahead and the girl needed some distraction to take her mind off Jatin's imminent departure.

Mrs Majumdar made a swatting gesture in her direction, as though she were a fly and grumbled…

"You are no good, Aditi. Have you ever packed a suitcase before? You will only make a mess of things."

Aditi surveyed the humongous mess in the room and exchanged a look with Jatin, who was lounging at a corner of the bed with a book in his hands which he had been unable to concentrate on.

"I have to leave the house in two more hours for the train station if I am to catch the seven o'clock train to Calcutta," he said to Mrs Majumdar, putting the book aside and stretching his body.

Aditi looked at the clock once again and gave Jatin a startled look. Their eyes met across the room and he got up from the bed putting his feet in to his slippers.

"I am going out for some time. I'll be back in an hour."

"Out?" asked Mrs Majumdar, looking up from one of the overfilled suitcases that she was presently struggling to close. She cast Aditi an accusatory glance as she watched her son's back retreat out of the room.

"You will be late if you go out now, Jatin. Could you not listen to me for once?"

"I'll be back soon!" shouted Jatin.

Seeing the thunderous look on Mrs Majumdar's face, Aditi promptly turned and followed Jatin with a hurried, "Mashima, I will be back soon too."

Jatin sat on a bench in the secluded park and waited for Aditi to arrive. He had no doubt that she would follow him there from the house. It was the spot where they had spent innumerable afternoons together during their long, languid childhood which had seemed unending until a few short weeks ago. A sound of pattering footsteps made him look up to see Aditi standing near the entrance of the park, looking around her as she desperately searched for him. Her eyes fell on him and she doubled down in obvious relief, putting her hands on her knees to catch her breath. Jatin walked over and stood before her with his arms crossed across his chest and his expression neutral, waiting for her to get her breath back. When she stood up straight again, he saw that her face was red, her hair had come loose, making her wild locks flow madly around her shoulders and there were lines of perspiration running down the side of her face which she wiped away with her dupatta.

"Aditi…"

She looked up at him and Jatin could see the unspoken agony that she felt, reflected in her eyes. He put his arm around her shoulders and led her towards the bench in the corner of the park. The sultry air of the summer evening hung between them like a barrier as they sat next to each other, and for once, neither of them knew what to say to the other. A sudden whiff of breeze arrived causing the leaves in the trees above to sway with relief, and acting on cue, Jatin closed the gap between them to wrap her in his arms.

"Say something. Anything," he whispered to her downturned face. "Speak with me; fight with me like you always do. Do anything, Aditi, but I cannot take your silence."

She opened her mouth to speak, but no words would come out. Her face was inches away from his and he leaned forward to kiss her. She reciprocated passionately, channeling her unspoken words into the kiss, and the barrier between them dissolved. Tears that she had been holding back began to flow down her face.

Jatin wiped them away.

"Don't cry, Aditi. I feel very guilty when you do."

"I am scared," she whispered, finally finding her voice.

"Scared?" he looked surprised. "Of what?"

"I am scared that you will forget me once you leave Burdwan. I am scared of not being able to compete with your dreams. It scares me because I cannot understand your dreams, and although I know you so well, sometimes, I still cannot understand you, Jatin. And I am scared because I do not know how to live without you."

Jatin was silent. The truth was that he had never thought about the consequences of his decisions on Aditi. In his head, he had always lived his life in the future which had seemed to hold a promise of being brighter than his present, and in his haste to reach that elusive dream, he failed to see the promise of true love which sat right before him.

"Aditi," he said, "do you trust me?"

She nodded.

"Then, all you need to do is wait for some time. You are the only reason for me to return to Burdwan and I want you to trust me that I will come back when the time is right."

He could see that the uncertainty was killing her.

"I will write letters to you," he offered, aware of how lame he sounded, "and I will also—"

"Take me with you, Jatin," said Aditi, grabbing his hands. "I don't care where we live as long as I am with you. Please take me with you."

It was at times like these when Jatin felt that he did not deserve to be loved in the way that Aditi loved him. At once he felt gratitude towards her, as well as a huge sense of responsibility of being able to live up to the pedestal on which she insisted on putting him. He shivered a little as he felt a subconscious fear that he would let her down. It was not lost on Aditi, who kissed him gently.

"Forget what I said. When you come back, you will find me waiting for you," she whispered and Jatin could feel the sting of tears in his eyes. She stood up and tugged at his arm.

"Let's go back home now or you will miss your train. Come on, Jatin. It's time for you to leave."

Four

Calcutta was fabulous. The city of joy. The cultural epicentre of the country which consisted of people who had a great love for good food, parties and entertainment. Pubs and nightclubs dotted the famous Park Street area which was considered to be the heart of the city. While most other states in the country were fighting to prohibit alcohol, Calcutta remained well-known for its colourful nightlife.

Jatin set foot on Howrah station on a hot summer night with three suitcases in his hands, a spring in his step and dreams in his eyes… like millions of others before him. He had visited Calcutta on a few occasions before, as a child, and the city with its wide streets, colourful buses, yellow taxis and trams seemed to belong to a different world. He boarded a bus outside the train station and through the ride, he looked out of the window in wonder, at the throngs of people who were still up and about, despite the late hour. Twenty minutes later, the bus dropped Jatin outside the gates of Nilratan Medical College. He made his way through the campus, marvelling at the large buildings which housed various departments and arrived at the hostel building. A jaded-looking middle-aged man who introduced himself as Bhola da helped him complete the formalities of filling in the requisite forms and then pointed him towards the first-year wing in the residential block of the hostel. The room where he was to stay was situated on the first floor of the four-storey hostel building. It was a small one where the only pieces of furniture were a bed and a wooden cupboard. The other amenities consisted of a bathroom at the far end of the corridor and a canteen downstairs. Jatin could not complain, since the hostel accommodation had come at a subsidised cost which fit in well with the meagre stipend that he was to receive as a part of his scholarship.

If the hostel facilities were not much to talk about, then the classrooms and laboratories for the first-year students more than made up for it. Jatin found himself immensely enjoying the course-work. His inherent interest made the subjects come easily to him and he spent hours in the college library every evening after classes, to learn as much as he could.

It had been a week after he had arrived in Calcutta. One evening, as Jatin exited the library and began to walk towards the hostel building, he could sense a group of senior boys follow him down the path. It was after dark and the campus was secluded at this time. Having heard horror stories about ragging incidents in the college before, Jatin quickened his pace, but soon the boys closed in on him. One of them blocked his way and the others flanked him on either side, making escape impossible. There were five boys in all. The one who seemed to be the leader of the gang, came forward and placed an arm around Jatin's shoulder. He towered well over Jatin, at close to six feet, was well-built and had a bearded face. He was dressed in a checkered shirt that was unbuttoned upto his waist and trousers, making Jatin feel conscious about the traditional white-coloured *kurta-pyjama* that he usually wore.

"Hey! Look who we have here!" shouted the boy to his friends. "Our bright, scholarship student! The only one this year. Can you imagine our good fortune to have the opportunity to be in his presence?"

The other four nondescript boys sniggered as they circled Jatin, like predators around a prey.

"Please get out of my way. I have to reach the hostel," said Jatin, putting on a brave face, although he could feel his heart beat rapidly within. It did not take him long to realise that he had made a mistake.

"What did you say?" barked one of the boys, grabbing him by the collar. "Did you just tell us what to do?"

Acting out of a primal instinct, Jatin pushed the boy back. This obviously enraged him further and before Jatin could do anything more, the boy had covered his mouth to stop him from shouting for help while the other four lifted him off the ground. Panic gripped Jatin and he struggled hard against their firm grip to break free, but he was outnumbered five to one. The boys carried him away through a hole in the adjoining college wall to reach a dark, remote spot behind the campus. A cold feeling of terror settled in Jatin's heart as he looked at his surroundings when the boys finally put him down. The leader of the gang, whom the others called Neeraj, grasped him by the shoulders and pinned him against the wall.

"You small-town bastard," he hissed in to Jatin's face. "Get it into your head that we make the rules in this college and if you are to stay here, then you will do as we say."

Jatin glared at him although he forced himself to stay silent.

"Lower your eyes," commanded Neeraj, locking his eyes into Jatin's and pressing down harder on his chest, "and say 'sorry sir'."

Jatin clenched his jaws together and said nothing. He fought the urge to spit into Neeraj's face. One of the other boys came forward and slapped him hard across the face so that Jatin could feel the salty taste of blood in his mouth.

"Do as you are told, otherwise..."said the boy in a menacing tone.

"Otherwise what?" Jatin shot back, still defiant.

"He's a tough one," said the boy to Neeraj, who said nothing but extracted a pen from his pocket and inserted it between Jatin's index and middle fingers, making him wonder what was about to happen. Before Jatin could think further, Neeraj pressed down hard on his fingers, causing an unbearable pain to shoot all the way up to his shoulder. Jatin gasped out aloud as he stared at Neeraj in disbelief.

"Lower your eyes," repeated Neeraj again, and this time, Jatin obeyed.

"That's better, although I did not hear the 'sorry'..."

He pressed down once more and Jatin cried out in pain.

"Sorry sir..."

Neeraj released his grasp on Jatin, seeming appeased for the moment. Jatin wiped the blood off his mouth and watched the boys out of the corner of his eye. His mind worked furiously as he tried to think of a way to escape when one of the boys lit a cigarette and held it out to Jatin.

"Here, take a puff!"

Jatin had never smoked before, but he did as as he was told to avoid further torture. Being inexperienced, he took a long pull at the cigarette which caused the smoke to fill his windpipe leading to a violent coughing fit. The others broke out into shouts of laughter while Jatin struggled to get his breath back. They waited for his coughs to subside and once again stuffed the cigarette in his mouth. This time, Jatin was more careful. He took a smaller puff and could feel the smoke glide past his windpipe to fill his lungs. After he had taken several such puffs, the boy backed away from him.

"Can I go now?" asked Jatin, keeping his eyes lowered. "I have done everything that you said, sir..."

The victim-abuser dynamic of the relationship had been established.

"We've only just started with you," said one of the boys. "It's only nine o'clock. Are you sleepy already? Do people in your town sleep at nine?"

Jatin said nothing.

"Okay!" said Neeraj suddenly. "Okay! We will let you go if you do something for us."

He had a snigger on his face.

"What?" asked Jatin, eyeing him cautiously.

"Strip!"

Jatin stared. He had surely heard him wrong.

"What?"

"You heard me. Strip! Take off your fancy dress and then we will let you go."

Jatin began to feel hot around the collar. He desperately looked around the secluded spot that they were in to see if there were any people whom he could shout out to for help. But as he had feared, there was no one around. He realised that no one would even hear him if he were to shout. His mind had stopped working. He pushed past the boys and made a desperate dash towards the college grounds, but Neeraj put out a foot to trip him over, making Jatin fall face down into the muddy ground.

"Get up!"commanded Neeraj, kicking him hard on the side of his stomach. Jatin winced in pain and raised himself to a standing position.

"Are you an idiot? You are not very bright for a scholarship student! Do you not see that you are only making things worse for yourself?" Neeraj hissed. "Do as I say. Take off your clothes or we will take them off for you. The choice is yours."

Jatin blinked back the tears that had sprung up in his eyes as he realised that he had no way out. He raised the kurta over his head and took it off to expose his bare chest. Although he kept his eyes lowered, he could hear the boys snigger.

"The pyjamas have to come off too," said Neeraj, his voice steely cold, "go on…"

Jatin untied his pyjamas and let them drop to the ground suppressing the natural urge to cover himself with his arms. This time the boys broke out in to shouts of laughter.

"Take off your underwear too," barked Neeraj. "What are you? A fucking bride? I asked you to strip. You know what that means."

Jatin hooked his fingers in his briefs and lowered them to the ground so that he now stood completely naked before the boys. He kept his head lowered as their guffaws reached his ears. Hot tears flowed down his cheeks. His humiliation was complete.

Five

Jatin had been unable to tell anyone about the ragging incident. The feeling of shame haunted him and it grew each time he crossed Neeraj or his friends in the campus or the hostel corridors. He had begun to avoid staying outside his room after dark and tried to stay close to the other first year students who usually stayed in herds to avoid similar assaults by the seniors.

Three days had passed by uneventfully, but on the fourth day, when Jatin was up studying in his room, he heard a sharp knock on the door. He froze. The watch showed that it was past eleven o'clock.

"Who is it?" he called out.

"Open the goddamn door or we will break it down!" came the response from outside. Jatin recognised Neeraj's voice instantly. It was a voice that he would never forget for as long as he lived.

For a few moments, he sat paralyzed with fear until Neeraj shouted once more...

"Did you not hear me? Open up now or I will break your door down!"

Jatin jumped up and no sooner had he unlocked the door, it flung open. Neeraj and his cronies entered the room, pushing him aside. He cringed in the corner behind the door as his mind worked furiously while he tried to think of an escape route. Neeraj grabbed him by the collar and Jatin saw that his eyes were red and his breath reeked of alcohol while he held a half-empty bottle of the liquid in his hand.

"First year students are not supposed to lock their doors," he hissed at Jatin. "Every student in this college knows this rule. I am sure that you did too. But you chose to ignore it. Now that you have broken our rule, you must be punished for it."

"Sorry sir," muttered Jatin, keeping his eyes lowered.

He could see some of the other first year students in the wing peer out of their rooms at the sound of the ruckus. They quickly receded into their rooms at the sight of Neeraj and his friends. The ground rules were clearly established. The college was Neeraj's fiefdom and no one messed with him.

Neeraj grabbed Jatin's face between his thumb and index finger, forcing him to open his mouth and pushed the bottle of alcohol in.

"Drink!" he commanded and Jatin gulped down the liquid, which immediately burned his throat and insides. He doubled down placing his hands on his thighs, gasping as he fought the swimming sensation that he felt in his head. Neeraj grabbed him by the hair to pull him into a standing position and pressed the bottle into his mouth again.

"Hey Neeraj!" said one of the cronies. "Look! He is drinking the alcohol that we bought with our money. He should pay for it."

"Fancy Dress is a rich boy. He gets a monthly stipend from the Government of India, no less!" replied Neeraj, sarcasm dripping from his voice. "He will give it to us… won't you?"

The meagre stipend was all that Jatin had to get by and between his fear of the bullies and his desperation for survival, the latter won.

"I need the stipend money for my expenses," he replied, averting his eyes. "I work hard to earn it—"

He felt a hard slap across his face which, coupled with his disorientation from the effects of the alcohol, made him fall to the floor. Before he could rise up, two of the boys pinned him down while Neeraj walked over to the cupboard and threw it open, rummaging amongst his neatly-arranged clothes and books and scattering them around the room. Jatin looked on helplessly from where he lay as Neeraj eventually discovered the small pile of his stipend money and turned to Jatin with a triumphant smile on his face. Neeraj leaned down towards him and waved the money in his face.

"Thanks for this. We will be back when we need more money, now that we know where to find it."

Jatin could feel his temper rise, and despite the warning bells in his head, he spat in Neeraj's face. There was a stunned silence for a few moments in the room as everyone, including Jatin, waited for Neeraj's reaction with bated breath. Neeraj straightened, wiped his face with the back of his hand and placed his foot on Jatin's chest, pressing down hard.

"You will regret this day, Jatin. I will make sure that you do. You still have not realised that you cannot survive in this college without our support."

Unable to move, Jatin turned his face away. Neeraj removed the foot from his chest, kicked him aside and turned towards his cronies – "Come on guys! It's time for us to leave now. We can come back later."

Jatin lay on the floor, with his hand on his chest, panting to get his breath back as he watched the boys disappear into the corridor outside, carrying all his money with them.

When he looked back on his life during the later years, Jatin could always point to a particular day in early October when a series of events began which had caused his life to quickly spiral out of control. It was precisely the day after their first term examinations had concluded; three months after he had left home.

During these months, Jatin had neither returned home for a visit nor had he communicated with his father. The silence at the other end was equally deafening. Durga Puja had come and Jatin had remained cooped in his hostel room while the rest of the city had erupted in joyous celebrations during those five days. He had of course received letters from Aditi, who loyally wrote to him every week, telling him about how her Durga Puja celebrations felt incomplete without him by her side. He wrote back to her with equal enthusiasm, describing the details of his life in Calcutta. He told her about the lively college campus, the huge classrooms and the fascinating laboratories. He told her about his small hostel room and about the terrible canteen food. He told her how he missed her bringing him his favourite food and how he missed seeing her every morning. He told her about everything except about the ragging incidents which overwhelmed him with a deep sense of shame each time he thought about them. It was seared in his mind that everything that was happening to him was a result of his inadequacies and he kept all of those stories buried deep within.

It was past eight in the evening. Jatin sat writing a letter to Aditi when the door flung open and Neeraj and his gang entered the room. By now Jatin was used to them coming to his room whenever they pleased, as though they owned the place.

"Come on, Fancy Dress," said Neeraj, pulling Jatin up from the bed. "Let's go."

"Go? Where?"

Jatin was wary as he eyed Neeraj, who was visibly drunk, as usual.

"To Professor Ghosh's house," came the unexpected reply.

Professor Ghosh was their Anatomy teacher and Jatin could not imagine why Neeraj wanted him to visit the man's house late in the evening.

"W-why?" he stammered.

"Because you have to do something for us. You will have to enter his house and get us the examination answer sheets. Ghosh takes them home with him after the exams and if you look in his study, you should be able to find them. I cannot afford to flunk the exam."

Jatin's mouth hung open which Neeraj ignored and continued, "Everything is sorted. Ghosh lives in the street next to the college. We will take you there. He lives alone and we know that he goes out for dinner to the college canteen every night around nine o'clock. That will give you a clear thirty-minute window, during which you can enter the house through the back door which he always keeps open, and get us the papers. So come on!"

Jatin resisted.

This was madness. He could not do this!

"I won't do it," he said, looking Neeraj in the eye. "I agreed to everything that you asked me to do. I say nothing when you beat me and abuse me every day. I give you all my stipend money every month. But this, I will not do! I did not come to Calcutta for this."

There was a moment of silence during which no one in the room moved a muscle and then Neeraj lunged forward to grab Jatin by the cusp of his arm and dragged the protesting boy out of the room. Jatin struggled to free himself, however, the other boys grabbed him too and they half-carried, half-dragged him down the narrow corridor, as the other hostelers peered out of their rooms to see what the ruckus was all about. Jatin's eyes widened with horror as he found himself being dragged inside the bathroom which was situated at the end of the corridor. A first-year boy who was in the bathroom scurried out before the boys locked the door behind them. Memories of the first ragging incident in the secluded spot outside the college grounds returned and filled Jatin with a sense of panic.

"Let me go!" he begged as they flung him down on to the cement floor. "Please try to understand. Please don't make me do this. If Professor Ghosh catches me, then I will be finished!"

"You will do as we say," said Neeraj, his voice steely. "Come on guys! You know what to do."

The boys grabbed Jatin by his arms and pulled him towards one of the toilets. Before he could realise what was happening, they had pushed his head into the toilet bowl. The overwhelming stench made him throw up immediately and Jatin struggled violently to free himself from their grasp, to no avail. Neeraj brought his mouth next to his ear and whispered.

"Now tell me. Do you still say no or will you do as we say?"

"I will! I will!" cried Jatin, desperately gasping for breath. "Please leave me for now. I cannot breathe."

"Are you sure? Think about it once more."

"Yes. I am sure. I will do as you say."

"Guys, let him go!" said Neeraj, his voice quietly triumphant. Jatin could feel the hands that were gripping him loosen and he collapsed on to the floor, gasping to fill his lungs with fresh air.

"Come on," commanded Neeraj, kicking him lightly. "It's almost nine and I don't want to lose more time."

Six

Professor Ghosh lived in a gated bungalow in a leafy lane next to the college. Jatin and the other boys walked up the deserted lane to reach the gate of the house and peered in to the dark garden walkway. The only source of light was from a naked bulb that hung outside the front door. From where they stood, it was impossible to tell if anyone was home.

"Go on," said Neeraj, shoving Jatin towards the gate. "It's past nine. I don't want us to miss this window."

"But what if he is home?" asked Jatin, feeling terrified.

"He is usually out at this time, but you will have to hurry, otherwise he will be back," said Neeraj, pushing him towards the gate once more.

"And what if he comes back earlier? If he catches me, then I will be finished. Ghosh hates students. He is known to be a sadist," said Jatin, trying to think of ways to delay the inevitable.

Every passing moment made his sense of panic grow as all sorts of scenarios ran through his mind.

"We will give you a signal if we see him return," replied one of the boys, kicking him hard on the foot and making him wince. "We will whistle and you will have plenty of time to leave through the back door and hide in the garden outside. So go now and make sure that you come back with the papers."

Left with no other choice but to comply with the wishes of his tormentors, Jatin entered the unkempt garden through the gate and looked back to where the other boys hid in the shadows outside. He could no longer see them from where he stood. He realised that he was now on his own. He walked surreptitiously in the darkness and reached the back door which was unlocked, as Neeraj had predicted. He gingerly opened the door to a crack and slipped inside the house to find himself in a dark room. As his eyes adjusted to the darkness, he took a look around the room to realise that he was in the kitchen. He tiptoed towards the door that led into the house when he felt something warm brush past his feet, making him jump in terror. He pressed his palm on his mouth to stop himself from screaming out aloud and looked down to see a ginger cat slink away into the shadows. He placed his hand on his heart to control its erratic beating and entered the living room. It was as unkempt as the garden outside, with books, clothes and unwashed plates strewn around the room. He continued towards the corridor that led inside the house and the first room that he peered into appeared to be the study. Jatin wished that he could switch on the light to see better, but knew that by doing so he would risk drawing attention to his unwarranted presence. He walked towards the wooden study table which had a pile of books and papers on it and observed the mess with a sinking feeling in his stomach. It would be impossible to identify the answer papers that Neeraj was looking for in the darkness. Although Jatin did not have a watch with him, he was acutely aware of time ticking on and he knew that he would have to act fast. Feeling desperate, he walked towards the door of the room and ran his hands along the wall until he located the light switch. He pressed down on the first switch, which caused the room to be illuminated and Jatin squeezed his eyes shut to allow them to adjust to the sudden brightness. When he opened his eyes again, he felt his heart skip a beat as he found himself looking into the face of Professor Ghosh, who looked back with an equally shocked expression on his face. Several moments of silence passed by before Ghosh broke the silence.

"Are you aware that trespassing is a crime?"

Jatin looked at the short pot-bellied man, taking in his bald head and thick mustache. Jatin could feel a cold feeling of fear settle in his heart. He gulped to clear his throat, nevertheless when he spoke, his voice came out in a croak.

"I… I can explain sir…"

"Please do," replied the man, crossing his arms across his chest and fixing Jatin with a glare from behind his thick glasses.

"I… I came here to meet you," he blurted, saying the first thing that came to his mind, only to realise how lame it made him sound.

Professor Ghosh took a step closer to him and looked him in the eye.

"I know you. You are Jatin from the first year class, aren't you? The scholarship kid. So, Jatin, tell me the real reason why you are here?"

Jatin looked away. He knew the consequences that awaited him if he were to tell the Professor the truth while he could only contemplate the consequences of not telling the truth.

"I will ask you only once more," said Ghosh, his voice sounding menacing. "Why are you in my house?"

Jatin bit his lip and remained silent.

"Okay. I have an idea," said Ghosh. "I think you are here because you want to steal your answer paper from my house."

Jatin grit his teeth, yearning to tell the truth, but he still remained silent.

"As I said before," continued the Professor, "trespassing is a crime and I am going to have to call the police."

"Police?" Jatin looked up sharply.

"Sir, no. Please sir," he began to beg as the enormity of the situation that he was in dawned upon him. "I came here because some senior boys had asked me to. I didn't come here for my answer sheets... Neeraj and his friends are waiting outside your house."

Ghosh's expression flickered for a moment.

"If that were so, then I would see Neeraj here instead of you, isn't it?" he replied after a moment's hesitation. "You see, I have no reason to believe you."

Jatin could see that he was trapped. He knew that all the teachers in the college were well aware of the way in which

Neeraj and his friends bullied junior students, but they all chose to look the other way for a reason which was unknown to him

"Sir, please let me go," he begged once more, folding his hands.

Ghosh shook his head firmly.

"I cannot allow you to get away with this," he replied. "If I report you today, then it will set a precedent so that no other student in future will ever dare to do what you have just done. Breaking into my house is unacceptable. I will also report this to the principal tomorrow morning."

The only thought in Jatin's mind was that he would have to escape. He realised that he was cornered and no amount of persuasion would help now. Unable to think clearly, he pushed the professor aside and began to run towards the front door. He felt a sharp blow at the back of his head, which made him fall to the floor as blackness spread before his eyes.

The sound of a loud rap before him caused Jatin to stir. It was followed by another one which was sharper than the first and it served to bring him back to his senses. He feebly raised his hand to indicate to the person before him to stop rapping. He could feel an excruciating pain at the back of his head which made even the simple act of opening his eyes seem painful. The rapping sound had mercifully stopped and he could feel himself drift back in to a deep sleep. No sooner than he had begun to relax, he felt rough hands grasp him by the arms and pull him up into a standing position, which forced him to open his eyes to a crack. He saw two uniformed policemen before him. His senses returned with a jolt.

Policemen? Where was he?

He looked around the unfamiliar, dimly-lit living room and tried to remember his whereabouts. As he ran his eyes around the room, they came to a halt on Professor Ghosh who sat on a sofa in a corner of the room, studying him over the top of his thick glasses. Jatin could feel his stomach fall out. The sight of the professor caused everything to return to his mind in a swift moment and Jatin realised that he had limited time to explain his presence in the professor's house. He opened his mouth to explain everything to the policemen, but before he could say anything, he felt a blow to his spinal cord, causing him to cry out loud with pain.

"Have you woken up or should I kick you again?" said one of the two identical-looking uniformed police officers. The men were still grabbing his arms to keep him from falling down.

"Stand up straight!" commanded the man, "... and follow us outside. You have to come with us to the police station."

"But sir, I can explain," said Jatin in protest, as the feeling of panic rose a notch higher. "I know that I made a mistake, sir. Please Professor Ghosh, I am really sorry sir."

The taller of the two policemen raised his fist again and Jatin held up his palms before his face in a defensive gesture.

"A mistake? Son, this will be one of the biggest mistakes of your life. In case you aren't aware of it, trespassing is a crime. And since the professor has put in a complaint against you, you are under arrest. Come on!"

Before Jatin could speak further, he found himself being dragged out of the house before he had had a chance to find his feet. Once outside, he looked around desperately, trying to locate Neeraj and his friends, but they were nowhere to be seen. Instead, he saw that a small crowd had gathered out of nowhere in the previously secluded lane, and people craned their necks to get a glimpse of the offender who was being arrested from the house of the respected neighbourhood professor. Ghosh stood near the gate, not taking his eyes off Jatin for even a moment. Jatin lowered his face to hide the deep sense of shame that he felt, as he was pushed into the back of the waiting police jeep like a petty criminal. The jeep took off towards the local police station and Jatin found himself seated in the back seat with the two policemen flanking him on either side.

The lock-up was a bare room with no piece of furniture in it and was divided into two parts, comprising a 'living area' where Jatin could count seven men who sat in close proximity to each other, given the cramped size of the cell, and the urinal at the other end from which an acrid odour assaulted his nostrils. There was a naked light-bulb hanging overhead, illuminating the centre of the cell while leaving dark shadows near the corners. The room had no windows and hence no ventilation, except for the air that came through the bars on the door of the lockup through which he was being pushed inside. Jatin knew that once he stepped over the threshold that was in front of him, then he would be locked in, with no hope of getting out until the police decided to let him go. He had no one whom he knew in the city that he could ask for help, and Jatin was too proud to reach out to his father in Burdwan. He remembered reading somewhere that the punishment for trespassing could range up to three months and could feel tears well up in his eyes. He turned around to face the constable behind him and made one last ditch attempt.

"Sir... please let me go," he begged. "I made a mistake and I promise that I will not repeat it."

The constable grimaced to reveal uneven paan-stained teeth and kicked him hard in the stomach, causing Jatin to double over in pain. Taking advantage of the situation, the man pushed him into the cell and slammed the door shut, leaving him to lie curled up on the floor, waiting for the excruciating pain to pass. When he could straighten up again, Jatin crawled on all fours to an empty corner of the cell with paan-stained walls and sat down, hugging his knees to his chest. The oppressive heat in the room caused a stream of sweat to trickle down his back, making his cotton kurta stick to his body.

He closed his eyes and tried to think of a way to get himself out of the mess that he was in. Instead his thoughts wandered and he found himself wondering about what his father would say if he saw him in this condition. He had fought the man and come over to Calcutta in the hope of making his future dreams come true. In his mind's eye, Jatin could imagine the look on Mr Majumdar's face as he would probably tell his rebellious son, that this is exactly what he had expected of him. And what would Aditi say? Would she still love him if she saw what he had become within a few months? He had come to Calcutta to make a life for himself, but instead, he had landed himself in jail.

How would he get out of here? Where would he go from here? Would this have an impact on his college education or on his scholarship?

Jatin had many questions but no answers, and could feel the throbbing of the bruise at the back of his head intensify. He thought of Neeraj and his gang, who had thought nothing of leaving him alone and running away when the police had arrived. They had promised to alert him if they saw Ghosh return and Jatin had been naive enough to believe them. Now he realised that the cowards had most probably run away as soon as they had seen the professor return. An overwhelming surge of anger shut down all other thoughts in Jatin's mind. He focused on the anger. He had always found this to be an effective way to stop himself from thinking about other things which were too painful to process. He thought to himself that he would make the bastard Neeraj pay for his actions on the very day he got out of jail. As these thoughts churned in his mind, he could feel the pain in his head and body begin to take over his senses. Jatin could feel himself drift into a deep sleep once more. He tried to fight the feeling of drowsiness for a while. A prison cell with seven other inmates wasn't exactly the setting where he wanted to be caught off-guard, but in spite of his valiant efforts to keep his eyes open, Jatin was soon in a deep, dreamless sleep.

A kick to the side of this stomach caused Jatin to open his eyes and look at the constable glare down at him. It took him a moment to get his bearings straight as he looked around the cell. The constable kicked him once more, bringing everything back to him. He was getting accustomed to the beatings and sat up straight, rubbing his eyes.

"Get up!" commanded the constable and Jatin obeyed to avoid further assaults. He wished he could kick the man back, but instead, clenched his fists and remained silent, wondering what more was in store for him

"Come on out. You are free to leave," said the constable, with a grudging note in his voice. There was no doubt that the man was enjoying kicking Jatin around and was disappointed by the fact that his joy had been short-lived.

Jatin stared at the man.

Free to go? Had he heard him right?

"Get out or I will lock you up again," barked the constable, beckoning towards the open cell door. Jatin hastily rushed out, following the constable into the front office of the Sealdah police station.

The man rummaged about an unkempt desk and held out a piece of paper and a pen towards Jatin.

"Here. Sign this! You can leave. Professor Ghosh is a kind man. He only wanted to teach you a lesson so we have instructions to let you go after keeping you in the lock up for one night."

Jatin hastily scribbled his signature on the proffered paper and exited the police station as fast as he could.

Seven

Jatin walked rapidly towards the college campus which was a five-minute walk from the local police station. It was the month of October and the seasonal rains had not yet abetted. A torrential downpour drenched him to the skin within seconds, but he did not notice it. All he could think of was to reach the college and confront Neeraj. The fear that he had earlier felt for the older boy had disappeared and now all that remained was a maddening rage. Jatin walked into the third year classroom and scanned the room full of laughing, yelling students until his eyes came to rest on Neeraj who stood near the window, smoking a cigarette with his back turned towards Jatin. He strode over, pulled Neeraj by the back of his shirt collar and began to drag him out of the classroom, unaware of the sudden silence that had come over the previously boisterous classroom. Taken by surprise, Neeraj was unable to respond until Jatin had brought him out into the corridor outside the classroom and had flung him down on the floor. He placed his knee on Neeraj's chest, making any movement impossible. He watched as the other boys' eyes widened with shock as he took in Jatin's appearance – his bloodshot eyes, his day-old stubble, his matted hair and his dirty clothes, soaking wet from being out in the rain.

"J-Jatin... how did you get here?" he stammered.

"Surprising, isn't it?" said Jatin, pressing his knee down harder on his chest. "How did I get here when you had arranged for me to be in jail?"

"I don't know what you are saying or what's come over you," said Neeraj, trying to push Jatin aside and sit up, but his move only served to enrage Jatin further.

He pushed Neeraj down and punched him hard across the face, causing blood to spurt out of his mouth. The sound of the slap ricocheted off the corridor walls and reverberated around for longer than it should have. Neeraj whimpered in pain.

"Now you can see how it feels when you hit others," said Jatin, unaware of the fact that he was shouting. "I do not understand how you can call yourself a human being, forget a compassionate doctor. Everyone in the college hates you, but no one says anything because they are scared of you. But let me tell you Mr Neeraj Agarwal, I am not scared of you anymore. You have pushed me beyond my limits and now you will see what I am truly capable of."

"You are not scared of me anymore, are you? You are quite the hero!" jeered Neeraj, baring his bloodied front teeth. He spat the blood out in Jatin's face and pushed him aside, taking advantage of his involuntary response. He stood over Jatin, swaying on his feet from the impact of the punches.

"You bloody small-towner. Can you still not see that you are finished? That your career is over? Go back to your town while you are still in a condition to return, or else we will…"

Jatin felt the blood rush to his head. He jumped up, grabbing Neeraj by the collar and pinning him against the corridor wall, before the boy could complete the rest of his sentence or react. Jatin raised his fist to punch Neeraj in the face when he felt someone grasp him firmly around the waist from behind and pull him away from Neeraj, who sagged down to the floor. Jatin struggled to free himself from the grasp and in the heat of the moment, he whirled around and turned to face the person behind him with his fist raised in mid-air.

Today he would stop at nothing. He would take on all of Neeraj's gang, if it were needed. Today he would make them all pay!

"Leave me alone!" he yelled. "This is between me and Neeraj and—"

He paused as he came face to face with the principal of their college, Dr H. Tiwari. The stern look that the balding, diminutive man gave him jerked Jatin back to his senses. He lowered both his fist and his eyes at once. At that moment, Jatin knew that Neeraj had been right about one thing…

He was finished!

Jatin paced up and down the small room outside the principal's office as he glanced towards the wall clock for what seemed like the hundredth time. During his four months at the college, Jatin had never been to the principal's office before and now, as he waited outside the room, he could feel his heart beat loudly in anticipation. The principal's secretary, Mrs Maity was an elderly, bespectacled woman who had been watching him in silence for a while and now she sighed aloud.

"Sit down, Jatin. You are making me feel sick with your pacing," she said. "They will be in there for a while now, so settle down until you are called inside."

"What's taking them so long?"replied Jatin irritably. "I have been waiting for over an hour now."

When he did not receive a response, he continued to pace around the room, sporadically running his fingers through his matted hair. He would tell Dr Tiwari about the whole episode, thought Jatin. Once he had explained everything, then surely, the man would see how he had been wronged. Jatin had always found it hard to articulate his feelings, so, in order to prepare himself, he had been running the lines that he wanted to tell Dr Tiwari through his head. Neeraj was inside and he had been joined by his father about half an hour ago while Jatin had just been asked to wait until he was called. He glanced towards the wall clock once again and sighed. Time seemed to have come to a standstill. He was about to tell Mrs Maity that he was going into the garden for a smoke, when the door to the principal's office flung open and Mr Agarwal stepped out, followed by his son.

Even at the first glance, Jatin could see that Neeraj had inherited his father's good looks, although Mr Agarwal dressed sharply in a suit and tie in contrast to his son's bell-bottomed trousers and unbuttoned shirt. The man paused for a fraction of a second before him, during which Jatin could feel that he was sizing him up, and then proceeded to walk out of the office. Neeraj stopped in front of Jatin, and placed his arm across his shoulder, which Jatin flicked off.

"Get ready to return home, Fancy Dress," he said in a low voice so that only Jatin could hear him. "And next time, be careful about who you mess with."

He patted Jatin on the back and disappeared from sight after his father. The rage that Jatin had felt some time ago returned and he contemplated following Neeraj outside when he heard Mrs Maity call out to him. It was finally his turn to meet with the principal.

The office was a big airy one, which was sparsely furnished with a wooden sofa set and a centre table which was situated next to the door. A large oakwood table with neatly arranged papers and folders was located at the far end of the room. The great masters of the medical profession stared down at Jatin from framed photographs on the walls of the room as he entered the office. The intent to intimidate a first time visitor to the office was effectively achieved.

Jatin walked in and came to halt before the desk where Dr Tiwari sat. The table dwarfed the man behind it even further.

"Good evening, sir," he said politely, but received no response.

He watched silently as Dr Tiwari took his time in carefully dipping a Parle-G biscuit into the cup of tea before him and chewing on it, before proceeding to study Jatin from over the top of his horn-rimmed glasses. His gaze made Jatin aware of his shabby appearance. He had neither had a chance to change nor bathe since the previous night and he could only imagine how he appeared to the principal. Jatin's throat was dry and he could feel all the lines that he had rehearsed in his head disappear before the steely gaze of the principal. After a full minute's silence, which had seemed more like an hour to Jatin, Dr Tiwari cleared his throat and reached out for a folder that rested on the top of a carefully-arranged pile of folders.

"Jatin Majumdar," he said as he opened the file and flipped through its pages

"Yes sir," said Jatin, feeling that it was necessary for him to say something at this point.

"Hmmm," said Dr Tiwari, not looking up, "...so you are a scholarship student."

There was silence for some more time during which Jatin could feel his heartbeat so loud that he was sure that the principal could hear it too. He watched Dr Tiwari leaf through the folder in his hands

"So Jatin," said Dr Tiwari after what had seemed like an eternity. "I would like to speak with your parents. Could you ask them to come over and meet me here tomorrow?"

Jatin cleared his throat to get rid of the dryness. "Sir, I am from a town called Burdwan. It's a small town outside of Calcutta and that's where my parents live."

"I see. So you are alone here. Well, that explains it," said Dr Tiwari, slamming shut the file and flinging it on the table before him. He joined the tips of his fingers together and looked at Jatin for a while longer, Jatin felt that he would burst out of anxiety.

"You see Jatin, we do not accept this kind of behaviour in my college," said Dr Tiwari finally. "I have spoken with Neeraj and his father for a long time and Neeraj has told me in great detail about what has happened. Despite his several warnings to you, you went ahead with your insane plan of breaking into Dr Ghosh's house last night to steal the examination papers. You did not heed the advice of your seniors and when the professor caught you red-handed, he understandably handed you over to the police under a charge of trespassing. He was kind enough to ask the police to let you go after one night in the lock-up, which I am sure, must have done you some good. But you didn't stop there, Jatin. You came back to the college today morning and resorted to violence. The whole college has been a witness to your actions."

Jatin's mouth hung wide open.

"But sir, that's not what happened. Think about it. I am a scholarship student. I did well in my exams. Why would I want to steal my examination papers from Professor Ghosh's house?" he began to protest, but fell silent as the principal held up his palm.

"But sir," said Jatin again, seething at the unfairness of the situation that he found himself in. "You must hear my version too."

"Jatin, I am here to make decisions and not to listen to stories," said Dr Tiwari, his voice loud and firm, "and based on what I understand, I can see that you are in the wrong. You have broken several rules of the college, including getting violent within the college premises, indulging in criminal activities and attempting to mislead other students."

"Sir, Neeraj has been lying to you," said Jatin, unaware that he was sounding as desperate as he felt. "Please let me explain myself and then you will see—"

"Jatin," said Dr Tiwari, cutting into his sentence. "Listen carefully to what I am about to say. Mr Agarwal is an old friend and a trustee of this college, and today, I had to answer to him because of your unruly behaviour towards his son. Neeraj has been our student for three years now, and so far, no one else has ever complained about him."

Jatin lowered his head to hide the anger that had begun to bubble beneath the surface. He knew that he could not afford to lose his temper again and clamped his lips shut to stop himself from putting his feelings into words.

"Based on my investigation," said the principal, "I feel that the nature of your actions are very serious and being responsible for the well-being of the other students in this college, I will have to take necessary steps to have your scholarship terminated with immediate effect."

Jatin looked up in disbelief. Termination of the scholarship would take him back to where he had been four months ago. He would once more become financially dependent on his father. Jatin could only imagine Mr Majumdar's reaction when he got to know about this.

"Sir, you can't do that, sir. That's unfair!" he began to say, but was stopped once again.

"I haven't finished yet," continued the older man, raising his voice. "I will also have to make a decision to expel you from the course since we cannot afford the risk of a student tarnishing the reputation of our college with such unruly behaviour."

Jatin felt his stomach churn. Surely he had heard the man wrong. He couldn't be expelled from the college. This admission letter had been his ticket to escape from Burdwan. And now that he was here, now that he was so close to achieving everything that he had ever dreamed of, he could not allow Dr Tiwari to snatch everything away from him in a single swipe.

"Sir, you can't do that to me. Please give me another chance," he said out loud.

As had always been the case with him, Jatin found himself to be tongue-tied at a time when his eloquence was most required. All the lines that he had rehearsed in the room outside had evaporated from his mind and now Jatin could only beg the man for mercy. The principal appeared unperturbed. He stood up, pulling himself up to his full five feet six inches, and looked Jatin in the eye.

"You will learn that life rarely gives you second chances, young man. But you could try. I will not stop you if you want to go out and look for admission to other medical colleges in the city, although I doubt if they would accept you after you've been expelled from our college. Be sure to give it a try, though."

Eight

Jatin exited the premises of the famous R.G. Kar Medical College, jostling his way through throngs of happy, colourfully dressed boys and girls who hung around the college campus like he had been doing until only a week ago. Things had changed abruptly within a span of a few days, with this being the fifth college that he had visited for admission during the past seven days. Although every college was different, their response to Jatin's request for admission had been consistent. No college was willing to admit a student who had been expelled from the famed Nilratan Medical College on behavioural grounds. His dream of being a doctor seemed to move further and further out of reach with each door that was shut on his face. The confidence that Jatin had had with him when he had left his home in Burdwan had now completely deserted him in the face of constant rejection.

It was past five in the evening and as Jatin walked along the sidewalk towards the bus stop, he noticed that the lively city life continued around him in full swing. It seemed unfair that everyone was oblivious to his predicament. Buses and trams, which were packed to the brim with people, passed him by. There were a few rare cream coloured Ambassador cars on the road which gained envious looks from the majority of people who had to make do with public transportation. The sidewalk along which he walked was lined with street vendors who called out to the passersby, selling everything from fried food to toys to clothes. Jatin was however blind to his surroundings. The heavy realisation had begun to settle in that he had reached a dead-end and the only way from here was to return to the small town from where he had desperately wanted to escape.

It was dark by the time he reached the college hostel where he lived, and instead of going to his room on the first floor, Jatin continued to climb up the stairs until he reached the terrace of the four-storied building. He remembered the first time that he had been to the terrace. Back then, he had been disturbed by the fact that it had no walls surrounding it, making for a sheer drop onto the grounds beneath. Today, however, he welcomed this architectural flaw and walked over to the edge of the terrace to sit with his feet dangling down the side of the building.

He looked up at the pitch-black, starless sky and closed his eyes. He knew that he was defeated and that too within a matter of four short months. A chamber that he had pushed to the far recesses of his mind had come alive since the last few days. Today, as he sat alone on the empty terrace, he could hear the demons within knock so loudly on the door of the chamber that he felt compelled to open it to a crack. A crack was all it took and a deluge of memories and pain flooded out, overwhelming him. He saw his mother's face as it had been when he had last been with her. That had been nine years ago, thought Jatin, nine years had passed since he had lost her. The memories were fading fast and now, even though he tried hard, Jatin could not remember her face clearly. However, he could still remember how the touch of her hand had felt when she had stroked his hair to put him to sleep. He could remember how her voice had sounded when she had called out to him. He could remember the warmth of her body as she had held him close to her whenever he needed her. He needed her now, more than ever before, but she was gone. Memories of the small one-bedroom house where he had spent the early years of his life came back. Along with it returned the vision of his mother as she had been during the last few days of her life; frail and fading. He squeezed his eyes shut to chase away the memory, but the vision continued to haunt him.

He had been very young back then, but he still remembered the hushed conversations between his parents from years ago, as he lay still between them, pretending to sleep.

"I am very weak, Jahar," he had heard his mother say. "I need to see a doctor."

His father turned to the other side and grunted, "I don't have the money to spend on a doctor. Surely you know that? I wish that you would stop complaining, Sunita. I am fed up of you always whining about something or the other."

"Can't you see that I am sick? I have had fever for almost a month now and it won't go away. I don't have any strength left to work or to look after Jatin. I don't want to die. Please help me, Jahar."

Jatin could hear the crack in his mother's voice and he squeezed his eyes shut tighter to chase away the tears.

"Will you stop being so melodramatic? I am sure that it's a temporary fever and it will go away in a few days. Now let me sleep, Sunita. I am tired."

That had been how most of the late night conversations between his parents would end. A month after that, his mother was gone and Jatin could never forgive his father.

His life had drastically changed with his mother gone. Mr Majumdar had begun to stay away from the house for long hours as he slogged to make his law practice successful while Jatin was left alone at home after he came back after school. During those long, lonely days, he had only one companion, the young daughter of Mr and Mrs Sanyal – Aditi. She lived in the big house in the lane next to theirs and studied in the same school as Jatin. Every afternoon, as he reached home from school, Aditi would dutifully come over with a tiffin box full of warm lunch for Jatin.

"Eat all of it, Jatin," she said, sitting watchfully by his side to ensure that he did not throw the food away. Jatin raised the rice and chicken to his mouth and grimaced. His palette was used to eating the spicy food that his mother used to cook and Mrs Sanyal's cooking seemed dull in comparison.

"It's very nice Aditi. Say thank you to Mashima from me," he lied through a mouthful of rice and was surprised when the girl burst out laughing.

"You are such an idiot," she said, poking him in the ribs. "You can't even lie properly, can you? I can tell from your expression that you hate the food. Don't worry, from tomorrow onwards, I will make sure that it's made spicy. Just the way you like it."

Jatin eyed her gratefully. She always seemed to know what he needed, even when he did not tell her. He finished eating and got up to wash his hands.

"Go home," he said to Aditi over his shoulder. "It's almost evening and your mother must be looking for you. You know that your parents don't like you coming over to meet me…"

She busied herself with washing up his plate and dishes at the sink, ignoring his words. Jatin silently thanked her because although he would never admit it to anyone, but the truth was that he was scared of being alone in the house with only memories of his dead mother for company. Aditi would stay back to keep him company every evening until the time that Mr Majumdar reached home. Later on, whenever Jatin looked back to those years of his life, he knew that he would not have survived without her.

Time passed by and a year later, Jatin's life changed again. His father was now a successful man and had managed to earn a lot of money. He used that money to build a spacious house in the vacant plot of land next to the Sanyal house and soon Jatin and his father moved out of the cramped one-bedroom house that Jatin so hated. However, along with the new house, Mr Majumdar also got himself a new wife who was about ten years younger than him. He had returned home one evening, later than usual, accompanied by a woman and an older man. On seeing Mr Majumdar and his guests, Aditi bid a hasty goodbye to Jatin and exited through the front door.

Knowing that his father did not like him to speak with his guests, Jatin was about to head towards his corner of the room when Mr Majumdar called out to him, "Jatin, come here! I would like you to meet someone."

The young boy came forward and obediently stood next to his father.

"This is Aparna and this is her father, Mr Banerjee," said Mr Majumdar and then he turned towards the guests and said, "...this is Jatin, my son."

Jatin folded his hands in a namaskar towards the strangers, like his mother had taught him to do. He noted that Aparna had a kind face and was dressed in a cotton saree, not unlike how his own mother used to dress. She came towards him and ruffled his curly hair.

"How are you, Jatin?" she asked.

Before he could answer, Mr Majumdar answered Jatin's unspoken questions with a single sentence.

"Aparna and I are going to get married next week, and from then onwards, she will come to stay with us. Jatin, you are to call her Ma and consider her to be your mother," pronounced the man, obviously unaware of the impact of his decision on his young son's mind.

Jatin felt as though he was being squashed under a pile of bricks. Hundreds of questions swirled in his mind; questions that he knew would remain unanswered forever.

The new Mrs Majumdar arrived a week after they moved in to the new house. She worked hard and tried to fit in with the family. With her efforts, she managed to fill in the void in their incomplete family picture that hung in the large living room of the huge house. However, she could never fill the void in Jatin's heart, which remained as a gaping wound that he had learnt to ignore and push away during most days. Except for some days like today. The spacious house had only served as a reminder for Jatin to the fact that his mother had not lived long enough to see it. He remembered her during her last few days as she had held his hand and made him promise her that he would make a successful life for himself, that he would get himself far away from the small town and get away from the squelch of poverty that had plagued them back then.

"Ma," said Jatin as he stared into the darkness from the edge of the terrace of his hostel. "I have lost. I could not fulfill my promise to you. I don't know where to go from here. I am lost."

November was the month when winter began to set in, in the sleepy town of Burdwan. Temperatures dropped sharply, often all the way down to single digits, and the town's people preferred to huddle inside their houses to keep warm. Jatin arrived in Burdwan on such a cold winter morning and began to walk down the familiar path that led from the railway station towards his house. He had not informed anyone at home that he would be returning, not even Aditi. Neither had he told anyone about his expulsion from college. He would tell them later, he thought as he walked along, pulling his sweater closer around his body to protect himself from a cold gust of wind.

He turned into the lane where their house was located, entered through the gate of their house and knocked on the front door, as the hollow feeling inside him seemed to grow deeper. Mrs Majumdar opened the door, and although surprised, she welcomed him home warmly. In characteristic fashion, she began to fuss around him, making him tea and warming some water for his bath while keeping up a constant chatter. His father was nowhere to be seen and the dutiful wife informed Jatin that her husband would be down soon. However, the significance of his father's refusal to come down and welcome him home was not lost on Jatin. He met the man only during lunch later in the day.

Mrs Majumdar hovered around Jatin with a bowl of fish curry in her hands.

"Here, have one more piece of fish," she said as she ladled it onto his plate, despite Jatin's attempts to stop her by covering the plate with his hands. "Eat Jatin! Look at how thin you have become."

Jatin gave her a smile. He knew that she tried hard to make him feel loved, although both of them were aware of the fact that she would never be able to fill the emptiness in his heart.

"It's very nice," he said truthfully, "you won't believe how much I have missed your home-cooked food. All I get in Calcutta is that horrible canteen food."

Mrs Majumdar looked appeased and settled down in the chair next to him, watching him eat. Jatin kept his gaze lowered into the plate to avoid eye contact with his father, who sat before him at the other end of the table. He could feel his father's watchful eyes rest on him and he was beginning to suspect that Mr Majumdar knew him better than he had given him credit for. Jatin kept his head down and concentrated on extricating a fish bone from the surrounding flesh.

"So Jatin," said Mr Majumdar, breaking the awkward silence that had fallen over the lunch table. "How are your classes going?"

Jatin nodded in order to avoid speaking. So far he had managed to keep the facade of nonchalance on, but he knew that he could not carry on much longer. He knew that he was lying to his father and that made him feel like an impostor in his own house.

"It's good to see you, although we were surprised to see you at this time of the semester," continued Mr Majumdar, somewhat relentlessly and Jatin gritted his teeth, wishing that the man would leave him alone. "We had not been expecting to see you before December when you have the mid-year break."

"We have a short break after the first term examinations," replied Jatin, not untruthfully, "so I thought of coming over for a few days."

His father did not reply and Jatin focused on finishing his lunch as fast as he could, so that he could escape to the refuge of his room upstairs.

Nine

Jatin sat up in bed staring out of the window. The full moon shone brightly, casting its gentle rays into the room, although in his present state of mind, Jatin failed to appreciate the beauty of his surroundings. He had been forced to take the decision to return to Burdwan after all doors that he had knocked on in Calcutta had been slammed shut in his face. But after coming back home he discovered that facing his father and telling him the truth about his expulsion was harder than he had imagined. A battle raged within him, where on one hand he could not muster the courage to speak with Mr Majumdar, and on the other hand, hiding the truth and pretending that things were okay made him feel suffocated. He rubbed his face with his palms, trying to wipe away the tension, when he heard a light knock on his door.

"Jatin, open the door!" came a loud whisper from outside, followed by another sharp knock. Not expecting a visitor at this time of the night, Jatin rushed over to throw the door open to discover Aditi, who stood outside, covered from head-to-toe in a red shawl. Casting a surreptitious glance around the house behind her, he hastily pulled her into the room and shut the door behind them.

"Aditi! What are you doing here at this time? It's eleven at night," he asked as he looked at the familiar small face with twinkling eyes look up at him. "Did anyone see you come here?"

"Idiot!" she said, unwrapping the shawl from around her to reveal a white silk salwar kameez beneath it. "I jumped over the wall behind the house and entered through the kitchen door. Mashima always leaves that open."

Jatin smiled despite himself and pulled her close to him. She wrapped her arms around him and they remained in a tight embrace, neither being able to speak for a long time as they relished the feeling of holding each other after months of separation. As had always been the case, with Aditi by his side, Jatin felt that he could fight the world again. He buried his face in her hair and whispered, "I've missed you Aditi... I can't describe how much."

She pulled back and looked into his face, running her fingers over the creases of worry that still remained on his forehead. He lowered his gaze, knowing that she could read his face. Aditi said nothing, but once again, held him close to her, cradling his head against her shoulder. He lifted her petite frame off the ground so that her feet dangled in the air and carried her to the bed. He laid her down and looked at her face in the moonlight that flooded the room. He noticed the kohl that she had carefully applied to her doe-shaped eyes and the light lipstick that she had adorned her lips with. He ran his index finger over her lips and lowered his mouth to claim hers. She kissed him back slowly, without a sense of urgency, making him feel a little less empty and a little more loved. He could feel her fingers run through his hair and he reciprocated by knotting his fingers into her curly locks. He slipped his hands under her kurta and when she did not stop him, he pulled it over her head to remove it. He looked down, for the first time, at the perfect, shapely body that she kept hidden under the loose salwar kameezes that she wore and gasped at what he saw.

"You are beautiful, Aditi…" he whispered as he allowed his hands to run all over her, relishing her every reaction as he touched yet unexplored recesses of her body. "...tell me if you want me to stop."

"Don't stop Jatin. Please don't…"

He lowered his mouth to trace circles around her flat stomach and felt her skin quiver beneath his lips. She unbuttoned his shirt and threw it away, running her fingers through the smattering of hair on his chest. He held her hands in his and paused for a moment, trying to control that rapid beating of his heart.

"Aditi... if you want me to stop, then tell me now," he repeated hoarsely, but she craned her neck to kiss him on the lips, indicating to him to continue.

They took their time undressing each other and exploring each other's bodies, each of them delighted at what they discovered. They made love until the combined beating of their hearts reached a crescendo and Jatin could feel her soft body melt beneath his. They held on to each other, waiting for the erratic beating of their hearts to subside. Aditi rolled away from him to lie on her back, while Jatin lay with his face buried in the crook of her neck feeling her fingers run over the muscles on his back.

"Jatin," her voice was soft. "Is something wrong?"

He did not reply. He did not know how to. There was so much that he wanted to say, but the walls that he had constructed around himself years ago made it hard for him to articulate how he felt. But now as he lay next to Aditi, naked and vulnerable, he could feel that she was close to scaling those walls. He felt overcome with a sudden sense of panic.

Old defence mechanisms jumped into high gear and he replied nonchalantly, "I'm okay, Aditi."

He had intended for his voice to sound breezy, but the words came out only in a whisper.

"Jatin, look at me," she urged, refusing to back down. When he did, she continued, "I know that it's difficult for you to speak about how you feel, but can you try?"

He turned away from her and squeezed his eyes to shut away the tears that had sprung up in them. He had been taught that tears were a sign of weakness and he did not want Aditi to think that he was weak. But something in her probing eyes made him feel a sudden urge to share everything with her. He needed to speak with someone. He needed to let everything out.

"Tell me that you won't judge me, Aditi."

"I promise," she replied simply and the ease with which she said those words moved something within Jatin. He kept his face turned away from her and began to speak, telling her everything; every painful detail about all that had happened over the past months while he had been in Calcutta. She listened, not interrupting him even once, until his words had dried up and his coarse breathing had returned to normal. When he finally dared to look at her, he searched her face for the judgment that he expected, but all he saw was compassion.

"Aditi, tell me what to do now. I feel so helpless."

"Tell your father, Jatin," she said. "Tell him about everything that happened."

"But Aditi," he protested, "you know Baba—"

She stopped him.

"I know Meshomashai. And I know you too, Jatin. You do not realise how similar you are to your father. Tell him everything because you have no other choice."

Jatin knew that she was right. He had walked out of the house, accepting a challenge from his father to make his life on his own, and now that he was defeated, he knew that he would have to muster the courage to face the man. He lowered his head into Aditi's chest and she hugged him tight.

"Talk to him tomorrow morning," she said. "You'll see that finally everything will be okay."

Mr Majumdar was sitting on his favourite armchair in the verandah of the house, sipping at his cup of morning tea, when Jatin came out into the living room.

"Let me get you some tea, Jatin," said Mrs Majumdar, who was in the kitchen attending to morning chores. "Sit with your father outside, I'll bring your tea there…"

Jatin nodded at her. Even after all these years, he couldn't bring himself to call her Ma. He walked out to the verandah and sat on the vacant chair next to the armchair where his father sat.

"Didn't you sleep well?" asked Mr Majumdar, evidently noticing the bags under his son's eyes. Jatin said nothing. His mind was working furiously as he tried to piece all the words in his head together into coherent sentences.

"Jatin... do you want to tell me something?" asked his father after a few minutes of silence. "You look disturbed."

Jatin looked at his father in surprise. He had not been aware that his inner turmoil was so apparent.

"Go on," urged Mr Majumdar, "Tell me, what is it that's bothering you."

Jatin jumped up from the chair and ran his fingers through his hair in characteristic fashion, as he paced up and down the verandah.

"Jatin. Come and sit here!" said his father beckoning to him and Jatin obeyed. Mr Majumdar put his arm around his son's shoulder. "Tell me."

"Actually I had something to say… I mean… something has happened… I mean, it's not very important, but you should know and I meant to tell you yesterday when I came home."

The words were coming out in a jumble and Jatin stopped, studying his feet. Both men were silent for a while and then Jatin spoke again.

"I have been expelled from the college."

He said it quickly, in a single breath.

"I know," came the unexpected reply and Jatin looked up sharply in surprise.

"Y-you know?"

"Yes. I received a letter from your college informing me about your termination and the grounds for it."

"Why didn't you say anything when I came home yesterday?" he demanded his temper beginning to rise.

"Because I wanted it to come from you."

Jatin said nothing. He had lost and his father had won and knowing his father, Jatin was prepared for him to rub it in.

"Going to Calcutta, to the medical college; all of this was your idea and I had warned you about it," said Mr Majumdar. "I tried to stop you, but you would not listen to me, so I let you go, Jatin. You fought with me and thought that you could take on the world on your own. You needed to learn the lesson for yourself."

Jatin clenched his jaws together.

"Now that debate has died a natural death since the doors of medical schools have been closed on your face. So let's think about what to do next," continued Mr Majumdar, oblivious as usual, to the feelings of his son. "When I heard about your expulsion, I knew that as always, it was up to me to clean up the mess that you have made in your life. I spoke to some well-placed friends of mine in Calcutta. I put my hard-earned reputation on the line for you and managed to get you an admission to the college of law at Calcutta University, even though it is during the middle of the semester. You will not have to lose out on a year of education."

"Law?" Jatin looked at his father. "But Baba, I want to study medicine."

His father sighed.

"Jatin, don't test my patience. I allowed you to do as you pleased but you failed, and now it is time for you to face reality. You are not made for a hard life and I am tired of having to pave the way for you while you spend your time day-dreaming and blaming me for stories that you have built up in your head. Do you realise that you have been expelled from one of the most prestigious medical schools in the city? After that, it would have been impossible for you to get admission anywhere had I not intervened. I expect you to be grateful for the fact that you are getting an opportunity for a good education, under the circumstances. Besides, law is a good profession. I would know."

I would know too, thought Jatin bitterly. It's a profession which could not pay enough to revive my dying mother. He bit his lip and remained silent.

"So, I take it that's decided then," said Mr Majumdar, patting Jatin on the back. "I will arrange for your admission and you can leave for Calcutta within the next week. Also, since you have lost the scholarship, I will have to finance your education as well as provide for your monthly expenses."

Once again, it had all come down to money. Jatin hated himself for having to depend on his father, but knew now that his back was against the wall. He had no other choice. He jumped up and walked towards his room, passing Mrs Majumdar on the way, who stood on the verandah with one hand covering her mouth, hung open in shock, and a cup of tea in the other hand.

Ten

Jatin was back in his room. He sat on his bed, inhaling deeply as he fought to fill his lungs with oxygen past the constriction in his throat. He had never felt smaller in his life than he had a few moments ago, in front of his father.

"Jatin…" he felt a light touch on his shoulder and saw Aditi beside him out of the corner of his eye.

"Go away Aditi. Please," he breathed through gritted teeth. "Please leave me alone for some time."

She said nothing, but did not leave his side, just like those long ago days of his childhood. He ran his fingers through his hair and turned towards her.

"You know, I actually don't give a damn about what that man says or thinks about me," he began animatedly.

"I really don't care about him, but he has made it his mission to dictate my life. Does he have a right to do that? He never understood me; never even tried. And today, I could see that he was enjoying himself as he put me down. He enjoyed the fact that I was proved wrong once again. He never really cared about what I wanted."

His words came out disjointedly. His face was red and beads of perspiration were lining his forehead, although it was a cold November day. The suppressed anger of years bubbled to the surface and Jatin allowed himself to feel the rage that he had bottled up when his mother had died due to lack of treatment… when his father had turned his back towards the nine-year, old boy. Thoughts ran incoherently through his mind and he clutched on to the one that was topmost.

"Did I ever tell you why being a doctor is so important to me, Aditi?"

"Why?" she asked calmly, although she had heard the answer from him several times before.

"I want to be a doctor because when my mother died, I felt helpless. I could do nothing to help her get better and I had to watch her die. And then I had to live with the guilt that I had allowed her to die. When she was on her deathbed, I had promised her that I would get away from this town and be a famous doctor so that I could heal people. I studied hard, very hard, to make sure that I got admitted to medical school and got a scholarship so that my father did not get the chance to dictate my life. Being a doctor was my only goal. It was the only thing that motivated me to continue day after day. But now, that man has to take that away from me as well, just like he took away my mother—"

His voice broke and Jatin swallowed hard, struggling to control himself. He would not allow himself to cry.

"That man outside... he is a murderer; he killed my mother. He did nothing to cure her when he could have. He just watched her fade away as the days went by, and when she was gone, he did nothing for me. He just left me all alone in that horrible house."

Tears had begun to leak out of the corners of his eyes, which he angrily wiped away with the back of his hand.

"Day after day, I stayed alone in that cramped house while he was busy making money and finding a woman to replace my mother so that his life was complete. He never looked back. He never cared that I was scared. I was scared and lonely, and I needed my father at that time. I needed him to tell me that it would be alright."

Now the anger had disappeared and only the pain remained. Jatin no longer wiped away the tears that were streaming down his cheeks and Aditi pulled him into her arms, cradling his head against her chest. He held on to her tightly as the only anchor that he could find.

"It will be alright, Jatin," she whispered soothingly into his hair.

His body convulsed with sobs as each emotion that he had kept pent up for nine long years tumbled out in a hurry. The Jatin that Aditi held was no longer the arrogant, proud man who was in control of himself, but he was once again the lost nine-year-old child that she had first met. She held him close, allowing him to cry, waiting for the last of his sobs to subside and for his breathing to return to normal. She could feel his tense muscles relax and his body turn limp.

"Come on Jatin. Lie down," she said, moving his body to lay him down on the bed. He felt exhausted and did not resist.

"Don't leave me, Aditi. Stay with me for some time," he said grasping at her arm.

"I will stay with you forever," she said, lovingly stroking his face, "that's my promise to you."

She bent down to kiss him and he pulled her down, laying her next to him. She turned on her side and placed her palms on either side of his face, kissing his forehead, the moisture in his eyes, the rough stubble on his cheeks and the softness of his lips. He raised himself on an elbow and looked down into her face, tracing her features with his index finger.

"I love you, Aditi. I would not have survived without you."

"Sshhhh…" she said, placing her finger to his lips, "Don't talk."

He obeyed and bent down to kiss every inch of her body, revelling in the way in which she responded to his touch.

Eleven

A cricket chirped in the distance; the calm countryside spread out for as far as the eye could see and the star-spangled night sky above seemed to encompass the earth like a giant shawl. Jatin sat in his favourite corner on the terrace of the house, beside the huge water tank which served to hide him from the view of anyone who might decide to venture to the terrace. This had been his hiding place throughout his growing up years and even today. This remained the only spot that he liked in the house. It was his go-to place whenever he was either happy or sad. Today, however, Jatin was not sure about how he felt. All his feelings had been numbed. Over the last forty-eight hours, he had fought many battles with his father, where the headstrong Mr Majumdar and his equally headstrong son had been caught in a deadlock of opposing views regarding the latter's future. There had been heated arguments, raised voices and escalating tempers. Mrs Majumdar had tried to intervene between the two men with little success. Finally, however, Mr Majumdar's wish had prevailed since he had the upper hand in the discussions, given the fact that Jatin had lost out on the scholarship and was financially dependent on his father once again. Being forced to take his father's money felt like a noose being tightened around his neck. He was to leave the next morning for Calcutta once more; this time to study law at the University of Calcutta. Jatin took several rapid puffs from the cigarette in his hand and closed his eyes as he felt the fumes reach his lungs.

"Stop smoking. It's bad for your health," said a voice next to him which made look up, startled.

Aditi stood before him with her hands planted on her hips. She plucked the cigarette from between his fingers and flung it away. Jatin reached out to pull her into his lap.

"Where have you been for the past two days?" he demanded. "I even went to your house to look for you, but your mother wouldn't let me in. Where were you when I needed you?"

Before she had an opportunity to respond, he entwined his fingers in her hair and kissed her, relishing the softness of her lips on his.

"Why didn't you come to meet me, Aditi?" he whispered on her lips.

"I couldn't. Baba wouldn't let me come."

Jatin gave her a surprised look. In all his years of knowing her, he hadn't known an instance when Aditi's parents had forbidden her from coming to meet him.

"Why? What happened?"

She avoided his eyes.

"There's something that you should know before you leave," she said finally.

He gave her a questioning look. Jatin could see her discomfort and felt a sense of foreboding come over him. He watched her wrap and unwrap the end of her dupatta around her index finger as she usually did when she was worried. His heart thumped in anticipation. He clasped her hands in his to stop her from fidgeting.

"Aditi, tell me. What is it?"

She hesitated. Jatin could see her struggling to give words to her thoughts and found it strange. Eloquence had never been a challenge to the usually talkative Aditi. His anxiety went up another notch, although he clenched his jaws to control his impatience.

"Jatin, Baba wants me to get married," she blurted out at last, seeming relieved to have gotten the words off her chest.

Jatin looked at her with disbelief.

"Aditi, you know that we cannot get married now," he began. "Explain it to your father and I am sure that he will understand—"

"You don't understand, Jatin," she said cutting him short. "He wants me to get married to someone else. I couldn't come to meet you for the last two days because of this."

For the next few moments, the only sound around them was the merry chirping of the cricket in the background.

"Someone else? And you agreed to it, Aditi?" his voice sounded weird and high-pitched. Aditi said nothing and he felt compelled to continue.

"So the alliance is fixed? Where did this suddenly come from? Who is this person? Do I know him?"

Jatin fought to keep his voice steady. He was not sure whether he was prepared to hear the answers to the questions that he had just asked, but when Aditi remained silent, he felt a sudden flash of anger.

"I asked who is the person, Aditi!" he yelled. His voice echoed back at them from the silent countryside around and caused Aditi to flinch.

"S-Sandip Gupta…" she stammered. "You know him. He was four years your senior in school. He completed his MBBS this year and has got a job as a medical intern at National Medical College in Calcutta."

Jatin moved Aditi's body aside from his lap and jumped up. He stood with his back towards her, looking out into the darkness. His mind had stopped functioning and he felt a tight knot form in the middle of his stomach, making him want to throw up. Just when he had believed that he had reached the lowest point possible, he was made to realise that his life could spiral down even lower.

"Jatin," she placed a hand on his shoulder and he flung it away.

"Jatin, I have not completed what I came here to say," said Aditi, her voice low but firm. "So please look at me and listen to me."

She forced him to turn towards her and placed her hands on both sides of his face.

"I said that Baba wanted me to get married to Sandip. I did not say that I wanted to marry him."

Jatin pushed her away.

"Come on, Aditi! We both know your father. Do you think you can win against his will if he decides to get you married to someone else?"

"I know that I can't win against him," said Aditi. "And that's the reason why I need your help now. You are leaving Burdwan tomorrow. Take me with you, Jatin. It's the only way in which we can be together."

Jatin stopped and looked at her. He studied her anxious face for a few moments and then rubbed his face with his palms. His future was uncertain and he was financially dependent on his father. Under such circumstances, he did not know how to react to Aditi's proposal.

"It's the only way, Jatin. Trust me," she continued." You know how Baba feels about you. He has never liked you and he will never agree to have you as his son-in-law. He will never agree to get me married into a family that he believes is beneath his status. You and I both know that this moment has always been inevitable. It's only been fuelled further after your expulsion from medical college and your return to Burdwan. Baba wants to get me married as soon as he can so that I do not meet you again."

Jatin knew, what Aditi was saying was true. This truth had always lingered at the edges of their relationship with neither of them willing to acknowledge it, until it had manifested itself.

Being forced to face reality, he felt desperate. He did not want to lose Aditi.

"Aditi, I have no money. I will have to stay in a small, rented house in Calcutta. I am not sure that you will be able to stay there with me. You are used to luxury and I can't provide you with that. I need some time."

"Jatin, I don't have time," said Aditi looking him in the eye. "If you leave tomorrow, then Baba will get me married to Sandip. So, please take me with you. No one needs to know. I do not care for any luxuries as long as I am with you."

He heard the crack in her voice and felt her pain. He pulled her into his arms.

"I have lost a lot in life already, Aditi," he said, "and now I cannot afford to lose you too. But I cannot be selfish this time and think only about myself. I leave the choice to you. I am leaving Burdwan tomorrow. The train is at 7 a.m. I will wait for you at the station. But if you do not come, then I will understand."

"I will come," she said, hugging him. "I promise you that I will and I am sure that if we are together, then we will find a way to overcome everything. I have some money with me that I have been saving for many years for our future. I will bring the money with me too."

Jatin stiffened. Her offer stung his ego.

"Aditi, I don't need your money. You are all I need."

"Don't say no to the money, Jatin. It's mine and I have saved it for us. Perhaps someday you will be able to get into medical school again in Calcutta, and then this money will help you pay for the college fees."

The earnestness of her appeal acted as a balm to his bruised ego. She always knew how to make him feel better, no matter what the circumstances were. He hugged her again, feeling some of the weight fall away from his shoulders.

A sudden gust of wind caused Jatin to pull the black woollen sweater closer around him. The Burdwan train station was desolate on the cold, windy morning and as far as he could see, there was no one else on the platform, apart from him and a few stray dogs. He looked at his watch for the umpteenth time – 6.55 a.m. He impatiently shifted his weight from one foot to another and craned his neck to look for Aditi. The train was due any moment now, but there was still no sign of the girl. Jatin felt anxious as several unprecedented thoughts ran through his mind. He knew well about Aditi's obsession with time, and now, with every passing minute, Jatin's concern rose until he heard the distant rumble of the train approaching the station. He knew that he would have to decide quickly between leaving town without Aditi or letting go of the train.

The watch showed 7.05 a.m. Jatin stood on the platform watching the train to Calcutta pull out of the Burdwan station. He turned around lugging his heavy suitcase behind him and headed towards Aditi's house. As he walked down the familiar path towards her house while absent-mindedly kicking aside the dry leaves that were strewn along the street, his mind travelled back several years as he remembered a childhood game that he and Aditi often played… of racing each other from the railway station to the gates of her house. Creases of concern appeared on his forehead at the thought of her and he quickened his pace. It was unlike Aditi to not keep her word. If she hadn't shown up at the station after promising to do so, then surely something must have happened; something that was beyond her control. He opened the gates of the Sanyal house and walked up the garden pathway that led to their front door.

"Aditi!" he yelled looking up at the window of her bedroom that overlooked the front yard. Jatin was used to seeing Aditi's face at that window whenever he visited the house, but today, the window was shut and the curtains were drawn close.

"Aditi!" he shouted again, raising his hand to knock on the door.

But before he could knock, the door flung open and Jatin found himself in front of with Aditi's father, Mr Sanyal, who glared at him through his expensive pince-nez glasses.

"What is it, Jatin?" he demanded, blocking Jatin's way. "Why are you shouting outside my house?"

"Namashkar, Meshomashai," said Jatin hurriedly, folding his palms. "I want to see Aditi."

"No! You cannot see her now. She is busy. Please leave," came the curt reply.

Jatin's anxiety had reached its peak by now. He would have to meet Aditi. Seeing that it would be impossible to convince

Mr Sanyal to grant him permission to meet with his daughter, Jatin made a futile attempt to push past the man and enter the house. Amidst this small tussle, his eyes met with Aditi's mother who was inside the house, as always, standing a respectful step behind her husband.

"Namashkar, Mashima," said Jatin, not failing to notice for the umpteenth time that Aditi was an exact replica of her mother. "Please let me come inside and meet Aditi. I am very worried about her."

"We, her parents, are here to worry about her. Aditi will not see you, so go away Jatin," replied the woman in an uncharacteristic firm voice. Jatin stared at the otherwise soft-spoken Mrs Sanyal for a few moments and felt desperation rise within.

"Aditi!" he yelled again. This time, he managed to push past Mr Sanyal to enter the living room, where he had spent several pleasant childhood afternoons playing with Aditi.

"Aditi, where are you? Please come out!"

There was still no response. Aditi would have surely heard him by now if she was in her room upstairs, thought Jatin. He headed towards the spiral staircase with the familiar white wooden railings that led up to her room.

"Aditi? Please come out. I need to see you."

Before Jatin could put his foot on the first stair, Mr Sanyal grabbed him by the shoulder to whirl him around and slapped him hard across the face. The metallic rings on the man's fingers caused the skin around Jatin's mouth to break open, making a thin stream of blood trickle down his chin. The older man caught hold of his collar and pinned him against the wall behind.

"Get out of here, Jatin, before I call the police and get you thrown into jail!" he hissed. "I've heard that you've already spent some time in jail and I am sure that you wouldn't want to go back in again. Get this straight, Jatin – my daughter is getting married soon and we do not want her to see you again."

Jatin pushed the man away and wiped the blood from his chin with the back of his hand.

"Meshomashai, Aditi wants to marry me," he said looking Mr Sanyal in the eye, "...and she wants to come with me to Calcutta. I am here to take her and no one but her can stop me."

Mr Sanyal slapped Jatin once more, seething with unrestrained anger.

"You have the audacity to stand before me and tell me that you intend to take my daughter with you to Calcutta! Who do you think you are? You are a low-life scum, just like your father. Opportunists, both of you. I know people like you very well. You only know how to take advantage of people and you've done it all your life with my innocent daughter. But now, it's enough. Aditi will not see you anymore, so get out of here Jatin!"

"I will not leave until I hear it from Aditi's mouth, Meshomashai," replied Jatin, refusing to break eye contact with the man. Mr Sanyal was a bully and his experiences with Neeraj had taught Jatin to never back down in the face of bullying.

"We should never have let you into our house," shouted Mr Sanyal. "How could you mistake our pity for you as consent to run off with our daughter? Aditi will not see you."

"I said that I want to hear it from her mouth," said Jatin through gritted teeth. "I will not leave until she asks me to. Aditi… Aditi... where are you?"

Jatin pushed Mr Sanyal aside and headed towards the stairs once more and was unprepared when the man retaliated by pushing him hard. He lost his balance and stumbled to the floor, hitting his head against the cold marble in the process. For a moment Jatin saw blackness before his eyes and it was then that he heard her voice.

"Jatin, what is it? I am here."

He raised his head to see her standing at the bottom of the staircase, with her arms crossed across her chest, observing him calmly. She reached out a hand towards him which he took and raised himself to a standing position.

"Aditi! Where have you been? Why didn't you come to the station today? You have no idea how worried I was about you."

"Jatin, please listen to Baba and leave our house."

Her voice was steady, in sharp contrast to Jatin's who now stared at her with his mouth hanging open.

"Aditi?"

"Just leave our house and stop behaving like a child, Jatin," she replied, pushing him aside.

There was a shrill ringing sound in Jatin's ears as he stared at Aditi. He opened and closed his mouth, but no words would come out.

"You've heard it now, you piece of scum. Now get out of here," said Mr Sanyal. Although the man was, next to Jatin, his voice seemed to come from far away.

Jatin ignored him and leaned towards Aditi.

"You don't have to do this, Aditi. You don't have to listen to this man," he said, trying unsuccessfully to look into her eyes. "I don't know what he has told you, but I can assure you that there is nothing to fear. You have the right to live your life in the way that you want. Come with me. We will make a life together like we decided yesterday. Today, I may not have any money, but if I have you with me, then I know that I will be successful someday. We will be very happy together. Come on, let's go."

He grabbed her by the arm and began to pull her towards the front door, blind to the resistance that she put up until she pulled her arm away from him and pushed him away from her.

"Go away, Jatin! Did you not hear me? Go away! Don't do this to yourself. Retain what's left of your dignity and leave! I can't bear to see you in this way."

Jatin was too stunned to react. He reeled from the impact of her words and watched Aditi remove a thick brown envelope from the pocket of the maroon sweater that she was wearing over her standard salwar-kameez. She lifted his limp hand and placed it in it.

"Take this money with you, Jatin. It's for you. You will find it useful."

A rough shove from Mr Sanyal brought Jatin back to his senses.

"This is enough. I will not have you in my house for another minute!" he yelled. Now that you've got the money that you had come here for, leave our house. You've heard it from Aditi too. She does not want to be with you."

Jatin ignored the man, not taking his eyes off Aditi.

"Aditi, if I leave today, then I promise you that I will never come back again. So think carefully before you make your decision," he held out his hand towards her. "I am asking you one more time to come away with me."

She hesitated for a short moment during which Jatin allowed himself to hope, but when she spoke, there was a finality in her voice.

"Jatin, I do not want to be with you. So please leave. Don't make a scene. Take the money with you."

A fuse blew in Jatin's mind. For him the whole world had always been on one side of the scale and Aditi on the other. She had always weighed heavier than everything else. Her casual dismissal of everything that was sacred to him made him lose control. He flung the brown envelope in her face and lunged forward to grab her by the shoulders.

"Are you trying to pay me Aditi? For what?" he yelled, his voice breaking. "For spending time with you when you were lonely and your parents were too busy to give you any time? Or for loving you more than everything else in this world? What is this price for? You disgust me. All of you are the same. You only care about money and about your flimsy social status!"

His face was red and his breathing was laboured. He felt firm hands grab his , and this time, Jatin did not protest as Mr Sanyal dragged him towards the front door and pushed him face-down on to the gravelly walkway.

"Scum! I should have never let Aditi mingle with you. Don't ever come back here if you know what's good for you!" he yelled and slammed the door shut on Jatin's face.

Twelve

Jatin arrived in Calcutta for the second time within the gap of a few months to begin his five-year degree in law at the University of Calcutta. The campus was situated in the posh southern suburbs of the city at Ballygunge. The degree was one that he neither desired nor had his heart in. Jatin seldom found enough motivation to attend classes, choosing instead to spend his days lounging around the college grounds while observing the throngs of students that inhabited the lively college campus. He made no friends and had no one to talk to. He preferred it that way because he believed that he had nothing left to say to anyone.

The evenings were the time that Jatin had come to dread. He had nothing to do to fill the long, empty hours with and to escape the painful memories, both old and new. Jatin spent the evenings by walking through the city, watching the yellow taxis, the over-crowded buses and trams filled with harried commuters and the skeletal rickshaw pullers who ferried overweight men and women to their destinations. Within a month of arriving in the city, Jatin had already spent so much time walking its streets that he knew most of the city like the back of his hand. He would watch the evenings dissolve into dark nights and the bustling city life grind to a standstill. Jatin felt a sense of oneness with the city after the shops closed their shutters, the street lights had been turned off and the rest of Calcutta had fallen asleep. During such times, the city transformed from a lively circus into a desolate island where the only signs of life were represented by the homeless people who lay bundled on the street pavements and the occasional stray dog that ran around the empty streets.

Jatin lived in a one-bedroom apartment on the ground floor of a building that was within walking distance of his college. The room was sparsely furnished, with a study table, a single bed and a wooden cupboard. It bore an uncanny resemblance to the old house in which he had spent the early years of his life. There was an attached bathroom and a small kitchen, which Jatin seldom used. The house owners, Mr and Mrs Ganguly, occupied the upper floor of the house. He had a contract with them where they would provide him with two home-cooked meals every day. With such logistics in place, his life was far more comfortable than the one that he had been leading in the medical college hostel, but none of this could help alleviate the emptiness that he felt within.

After arriving in Calcutta, Jatin neither wrote nor received any letters – either from his father or from Aditi. He had expected none. Then, surprisingly, a letter arrived one morning with Aditi's familiar writing on the cover. Jatin eagerly grabbed it from the postman. Acting out of habit, he rushed inside the house and began to tear the envelope open to read the contents within when he stopped himself. He reminded himself of the promise that he had made to himself on the day that he had left Burdwan that Aditi was no longer to be a part of his life. He put the unopened letter away. Over the next few weeks, letters from Aditi poured in at regular intervals and Jatin stacked all of them away in a neat pile at the corner of his study table. Unopened.

Time flew by and soon winter settled in on the city. It was a cold night in December and Jatin was out on one of his nocturnal sojourns. He had buttoned up his woollen sweater all the way up to his chin and had buried his hands deep within the pockets of his patent cotton kurta while he wandered around Park Street – the heart of Calcutta. It was past one o'clock and most pubs were shut at this hour with only a few that remained open to accommodate the occasional late night reveller. The street was deserted and Jatin looked at the lifeless neon lights that usually shone brightly above the pubs that dotted both sides of the street. Without the bright lights, the glamorous pubs looked shabby and desolate. He walked along, following the tram line towards his house in Ballygunge.

He turned a corner into the adjoining Beniapukur area, which was a locality that amongst other things, housed the famed National Medical College. Getting admission to this college had once been a dream. Jatin came to a halt before the huge gates of the college, craning his neck to get a look inside. The campus looked secluded except for a couple of security guards who sat dosing on plastic chairs outside the college gates. He sat on the pavement opposite the campus and lit a cigarette. This was the only medical college in the city to which he hadn't ventured after his expulsion, given that it was the most reputed college in the city and the possibility of them admitting an expelled student had seemed to be very narrow to him.

And then all of a sudden, the stillness of the night was broken by the sounds of pounding footsteps. He looked up from his spot on the pavement to see a man run down the street, followed by a pack of four other men who were chasing him. It did not take the four men too long to close in on their victim and once they caught hold of him, they threw him on the ground and began to pound him mercilessly with their fists. The man lay on the ground and screamed out for help. Momentarily paralyzed, Jatin looked on in horror at the scene that unfolded before his eyes. He looked across the street to see if the security guards outside the college gates could help, but the men had disappeared on seeing the commotion.

"Help! Help me, please!" screamed the man on the ground as he struggled to free himself from the clutches of his attackers, who continued to beat him up relentlessly.

As Jatin watched on, the man managed to momentarily fend off the punches to his face and looked around wildly to seek help.

His eyes fell on Jatin who was standing frozen on the pavement. Their eyes met for a brief moment and Jatin could see the look of desperation in the man's eyes. He could see blood ooze out of his mouth, and in that moment, he knew that he could not be a silent spectator anymore. Just as Jatin was trying to think about a way to help, he saw one of the four men extract a knife from his pocket and stab the victim who lay on the ground. He shrieked out in pain. It was a visceral scream and Jatin realised that there was only one thing that he could do now, and he acted without any further thought.

"Hey! Stop it!!" he yelled.

His voice rang up and down the desolate street, startling him as well as the four men. They froze and looked up to see the young man stand a short distance away from them. Jatin looked each of the men in the eyes, hoping that the fear that he felt within did not reflect on his face and said in a firmer voice, "I said, let him go…"

The men did not reply; nor did they move. They looked uncertainly at each other and Jatin kept his fingers crossed, hoping that they would run away. He knew that he was not strong enough to take on the four of them if they decided to attack him.

He took a step forward towards the men and spoke again, "I said leave, unless you want me to call the police."

The mention of the police had the intended effect on the men. One of them, who seemed to be the leader of the gang, beckoned to the others. After kicking their victim one more time, the four men ran down the street and disappeared from sight. For the next few moments, an eerie silence descended on the street.

Jatin did not move as he waited for the rapid beating of his heart to slow down and then he heard the man who still lay on the ground call out to him feebly, "Please help me. I don't want to die."

These words galvanised Jatin into action. He rushed forward to kneel beside the man. He was bleeding profusely from a wide gash that had formed on the left side of his body where he had been stabbed. His mind worked furiously as he tried to draw on the few months of education that he had received at medical college. He knew that if he did not stop the bleeding immediately, the man would die. In fact, he could see him fading away already. He knew that he would have to keep him from losing consciousness, so he tried to engage him in a conversation.

"Hey," he said, looking the man in the eye. "What's your name?"

"S-Shyam," he murmured, closing his eyes again.

"Shyam. Look at me," said Jatin, gently slapping his face and causing the man to open his eyes to a crack. "Don't worry, you will be alright. What I am going to do will hurt a little but it's for your good. Is that okay, Shyam?"

The delirious man nodded slightly and Jatin pressed his palm down on his wound the way in which he had been taught to do in medical school to temporarily stop the flow of blood. Shyam shouted out in pain, his scream reverberating in the quiet surroundings and Jatin could feel his hands shake.

"I am sorry Shyam, but I have to stop your bleeding," he muttered

Keeping his hand firmly pressed down on the wound, Jatin looked around for help. He knew that next, he would have to get Shyam inside the hospital across the road and was relieved to see that the two security guards from outside the hospital had appeared again and were approaching them.

"Please help me carry him inside," he yelled to them. "Call a doctor. It's an emergency!"

The commanding tone in his voice made the men rush forward. They carefully lifted Shyam off the street while Jatin continued to press down on the wound. As they entered the hospital premises, a couple of doctors wearing white coats appeared from inside a building carrying a stretcher with them, on which Shyam was transferred.

"Let's take him to the emergency room. He needs stitches, but before that, let's put a temporary dressing on his wound," said one of them while the other extracted a thick white gauze from the pocket of his coat.

Jatin was still pressing down on the wound with his palm, thus managing to reduce the flow of blood. His hand was soaked with the red liquid, causing it to slip, but he managed to continue to press down until one of the doctors asked him to let go. As soon as Jatin had removed his hand, blood spurted out of the wound and the doctor rapidly placed the gauze on it. The white gauze turned red within seconds.

"My name is Amit, and this is my colleague Anand," said the man, briefly looking at Jatin. "We are medical interns at the college. Thanks for your presence of mind. It might actually save his life. By the way, are you related to this man in any way?"

"I don't know him. I only know that his name is Shyam. I just happened to be passing by when some men stabbed him and then ran away."

Amit and Anand exchanged looks and then instructed the security guards who were standing beside Jatin to call the police station. The guards nodded and disappeared from sight while Jatin stood by silently, watching as the two men began to carry the now unconscious Shyam inside the hospital. He was about to turn away, when Amit called out to Jatin over his shoulder.

"Don't leave yet. The police will be here soon and they might want to speak with you. In the meanwhile, why don't you come and join us in the emergency room? There aren't any nurses around at this time and you might be able to help us."

Jatin spent the next thirty minutes assisting Amit and Anand in the emergency room, handing them scissors and swabs while they sewed up the wound and administered painkiller injections. Fortunately, there had been no damage to any of his internal organs, and finally, Shyam was declared to be out of danger. The police arrived shortly afterwards and Jatin spent the next hour telling them all that he had seen. When the police seemed satisfied, Jatin was given permission to leave. He stepped out of the hospital building past 2 a.m., into the fresh air of the sprawling medical college campus. He was shaken beyond measure and lit a cigarette. He looked around the manicured lawn before him and wistfully eyed the college building once more, thinking about what could have been. He was about to turn around and leave for home when he heard someone call out his name. He turned around to see Amit and Anand exit the building and walk towards him.

"Hey Jatin! Come and have some tea with us in the canteen before you leave," said Amit. "You must be exhausted after the long night."

"We have a joke that our canteen makes the worst tea that you can get anywhere in Calcutta," added Anand with a laugh. "Come and see it for yourself."

Jatin joined the two men in the empty hospital canteen. They were all tired, but Amit was talkative. Jatin was tired and his defences were down. Also, this was the first time that he was speaking with someone since he had arrived in Calcutta a month ago. The words seemed to pour out and over tea, he told the two boys about his previous experience at medical college. Although he could not bring himself to tell them the complete story, he told them about the ragging incidents, his subsequent expulsion from the college and his inability to get an admission to any other medical college in the city. While he spoke, memories of the traumatic ragging incidents returned and Jatin felt a familiar hotness around his collar, as the potent mix of shame and anger returned.

"I had put all of that behind me, as a closed chapter in my life, until today, when I was assisting you guys in the emergency room. I realised once more that this is what I want to do. But…" he trailed off.

There was silence around the table for a few moments as Amit and Anand digested what they had just heard.

Anand patted Jatin on the back. "I have an idea, Jatin. Why don't you speak with our Dean, Dr Banerjee? He is a sympathetic man who truly cares for students and for the medical profession. If you tell him what you told us truthfully, then you might have a chance here."

Jatin sat up straight.

"Could you help me get an appointment?" he asked eagerly and then added with a touch of his standard arrogance. "After all, my grades have always been very good and I have been a national scholarship student."

Thirteen

It was past three o'clock when Jatin left the premises of the National Medical Hospital. After the discussion with his new friends, he could already feel some of his old fighting spirit return. Perhaps seeking an appointment at the college for an admission was not a bad idea. Of course, money would be a problem, but he would think about that later. After all, he had very little to lose. Jatin was lost in thought, taking several puffs from the cigarette that he held between his fingers as he walked along the deserted sidewalk towards his house. His mind worked furiously as he began to plan on how he would present his case to the Dean if he were to get an appointment with him. Lost in thought, Jatin did not realise that he had taken a wrong turn to veer off the main road and enter into a narrow alley. He looked up only when he heard a low rumble of voices and found himself in an unknown locality. He was outside a restaurant that was packed with people even in the middle of the night.

"Sir, welcome to Jimmy's. Please come inside, sir. Here, have a look at our menu," said a boy of about his age, who was wearing a dirty T-shirt and had shoulder length hair. Not waiting for a response, the boy thrust a laminated menu in Jatin's face. He scanned the same to realise that Jimmy's was a pub that sold local alcohol at prices which seemed to suit his modest budget. It was also one where his age did not seem to be a restriction as was the case with most of the upscale pubs in Park Street. It was just what he needed at that moment, thought Jatin! He followed the boy inside to see that the pub consisted of a dimly-lit room with thick cigarette smoke hanging in the air. The room reeked of cheap alcohol and fresh sweat. There were wooden tables and chairs scattered around the room and almost every table was filled with men of all age groups, ranging all the way from under-aged teenagers to men well into their fifties. Jatin slipped into a vacant booth near the corner of the room to ensure that he was inconspicuous and lit a cigarette. A while later, a girl who was scantily-clad in a short, low-cut top and a tight skirt, appeared before him.

"Good evening, sir. I am your waitress Rosie," she said by way of introduction and held out a replica of the laminated menu that he had seen outside. "What would you like to drink, sir?"

Rosie's face looked deathly pale in the light of the naked bulb that hung overhead. It was hard to tell the actual colour of her skin that lay beneath the thick layer of make-up that she had applied to her face. Her lips and her nails were painted a bright shade of red. Aware that he had been staring, Jatin hastily averted his eyes from her and scanned the menu that she continued to hold before him. His only drinking experience so far had been during the days that he had spent in medical college and he did not have a great understanding of the items listed on the menu.

His confusion must have been apparent, since Rosie added helpfully, "Let me get you our house special to begin with, sir."

He nodded and she disappeared to reappear momentarily with a glass bottle in her hands, which she placed on the table before him.

"Enjoy your drink," she said and was gone again before he could look up.

The rapidness with which she came and went made Jatin wonder whether she was a real woman or an apparition. He raised the bottle to his mouth, taking a slow swig from it. A warm sensation coursed through his body and he felt the tightness in his shoulder muscles relax. With each sip that he took, he could feel some of the tension fall away. Soon, Jatin lost track of time. Each time that he emptied the bottle before him, Rosie would reappear to refill it until he lost count of how much he had had to drink. The throbbing pain inside him dulled with each drink until he could feel nothing at all, except for an all-pervasive sense of numbness. He placed his head on the wooden table before him and closed his eyes.

"Jatin... Jatin. Are you okay?" came Aditi's concerned voice and Jatin cracked his eyes open to see his ten-year-old friend's face hovering over him. There were creases of worry

on her small forehead. His head was pounding and it felt as though it would burst; his throat was parched dry and his body felt hot.

"Here, have this medicine and you will be okay," she said, helping him up to a sitting position. He gulped down the contents from the glass that she held out to him and clutched on to the end of her frock as she was about to turn away from him. He was back in his one-room childhood home and he did not want to be left alone there. He was scared of being alone.

"Don't leave me Aditi," he mumbled. She extracted her dress from his fingers and helped him lie back down.

"I am here, Jatin," she said soothingly running her fingers through his hair. The anxiety dropped away and he drifted into a deep sleep.

When Jatin opened his eyes again, he was still in the one-room house, but Aditi was nowhere in sight.

"Aditi... Aditi!" he screamed, looking desperately around the empty room. His fever seemed to have disappeared and he jumped out of bed. He rushed out to the street outside the house to look for her. His mind worked on an overdrive. Where had she gone? Was she alright? He began to run towards her house, but he noticed that, strangely, with every step that he took, the house seemed to move further and further away. He continued to run until his breath came in spurts. But he knew that he could not stop until he reached her. And then, all of a sudden, she appeared before him. He came to a grinding halt. She stood with her back turned towards him, outside the gates of her house.

"Aditi!"

She did not turn to look at him but began to walk towards the house. Jatin ran after her until he was next to her and reached out an arm to turn her around to face him.

"Why are you running away from me?" he asked, looking into her twinkling eyes.

"Go away, Jatin," she replied, pushing him away. She thrust a thick, brown envelope in his hands. "Take this money with you and go away. I cannot go with you."

"Aditi... please don't do this."

He begged as he could feel someone's hands grab him by the shoulder and shake him.

"Please Aditi," he continued to mumble.

"Wake up, sir!" came a voice next to his ears. "It's time for us to close. You will have to leave now."

Jatin opened his eyes to see Rosie's face come into focus. The world that was in his mind dissolved and disappeared and he looked around him dazed, unable to recognise the woman before him or the shabby room that he was in. There was a tremendous throbbing in his head from the after effects of the cheap alcohol.

"Sir... here's your bill. It's time for us to close. It's six in the morning; closing time," said Rosie

Things returned to his mind in a jumble as he vaguely recognised the pub. He looked around to see that the pub was almost empty now and hastily rose to leave. He placed the money on the table and stumbled as he began to walk towards the exit. Rosie was by his side, placing a steadying arm around his waist.

"Easy sir. I can take you home if you like," she whispered to him. "You will have to pay me for my time, but I can promise you that I will make it worth it."

Although he was not in complete possession of his senses, Jatin still understood her proposition well and recoiled.

"Get lost!" he slurred, pushing her away in disgust.

She stood undeterred by the insult and looked him in the eye.

"Think about it, sir. I can be whatever you want me to be. I can even be Aditi, if you like."

It had been the wrong thing to say and she had unconsciously touched a raw nerve.

"How do you know about Aditi and how can you even imagine that you can be like her?" yelled Jatin. "Get away from me, you bloody slut! You disgust me."

He pushed her away and stepped onto the street, out of the pub, to walk back to his house.

Fourteen

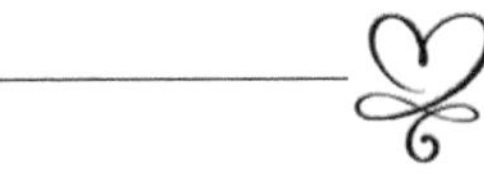

Jatin had no memory of how he reached home that day, but he found himself outside the gate of the house in Ballygunge where he lived. He staggered towards the front door to unlock it and noticed Mrs Ganguly peer down at him from the stairway above with a disapproving look on her face. He was too drunk to take note of her. Ignoring her, he stumbled inside the house once he had managed to unlock the door and headed straight for the bed at the corner of the room to collapse on it. For some time, his head swam as several images came and went at an alarming speed, making it impossible for him to hold on to any one thought.

Aditi, his father, Dr Tiwari, Neeraj, Shyam.

Images of blood spurting out of a wound swam before his eyes and he heard Aditi's voice ring in his head as she said – *I am scared of blood, Jatin.*

He squeezed his eyes shut tightly and placed his palms over his ears, wishing that the images would slow down so that he could go to sleep and forget everything for some time. He lay absolutely still for a while, not moving a muscle. The swimming sensation in his head mercifully began to slow down at first and then gradually disappeared, allowing Jatin to fall into a deep, dreamless sleep. It was the first time that he had slept since the day he had arrived in Calcutta over a month ago. His body was relaxed and Jatin felt as though he was floating through thin air. The usually hard pillow under his head seemed soft. It felt as though he was lying in Aditi's lap and she was stroking his hair, just the way he liked it.

"Aditi?" he murmured in his sleep.

"Jatin, Jatin! Wake up…"

Someone was slapping him lightly across the face and Jatin wanted to tell them to stop. All he wanted to do was to sleep.

"Go away!" he tried to shout, but the words only came out in a whisper.

"Wake up, Jatin!" said the voice. "You have been asleep for almost two hours. Open your eyes."

He opened his eyes a little and found himself looking into a pair of twinkling eyes. He shut his eyes again. *The damn dream was back. No matter what he did, it refused to go away.*

"Jatin, open your eyes! It's me, Aditi."

This time he opened his eyes fully and saw Aditi look down at him with creases of concern on her forehead.

"Are you okay? I've been trying to wake you up for a while now, and I was getting concerned."

He sat up straight in a swift motion, stunned to see her in his room. He immediately regretted the rapid movement as a feeling of nausea assaulted him. He rushed towards the bathroom sink to throw up, the muscles in his empty stomach contracting in protest. He splashed cold water on his face and kept his head lowered until the wave of nausea had passed. He straightened up to look at his reflection in the small mirror that hung above the sink and recoiled at what he saw. His eyes were bloodshot, his cheeks sunken and there was an unkempt beard that had grown on his usually clean-shaven face. A movement behind him caused him to turn around, bringing him face to face with Aditi. She stood near the door of the cramped bathroom.

So it had not been a dream. She was really in his house.

Jatin's instinctive reaction on seeing her was one of pure happiness. He had missed her far more than he cared to acknowledge, and after months of being alone, he yearned to hold her close to him. He reached out and hugged her tightly, burying his face in her shoulder, allowing hot tears to roll down his face. She hugged him back and the two of them remained in a tight embrace, neither wanting to let go of the other. In that small moment that they shared, nothing else existed, except for the two of them. It felt just right. Lost in a world of their own, neither of them heard the knock on the door. Another knock followed, louder this time, causing Jatin to break out of the trance. He reluctantly let go of Aditi and walked out into the front room to see a man at the door, who looked familiar. His presence in Jatin's house was so unexpected that Jatin was momentarily unable to place the boy. It had been several years since he had met Sandip and it took him a few moments before he recognised him.

"Sandip, isn't it?" said Jatin incredulously.

"Hi Jatin. Sorry to barge into your house in this way, but I was getting worried about Aditi," replied Sandip, sounding apologetic. He looked past Jatin towards Aditi who was standing behind and said.

"I am waiting for you outside, Aditi. Let me know when you are ready to leave. It had been a long time since you came inside, so I thought of checking in to see that everything was okay with you."

"I am okay, Sandip," said Aditi, seeming a little flustered. "Could you give me a little more time?"

Sandip nodded and disappeared, closing the door behind him. As the door clicked shut, everything returned to Jatin in a flash and the impact of the realisation was so strong that he felt as though someone had punched him hard in the stomach. He looked towards Aditi, who had come to stand before him. The feeling of betrayal returned and although Jatin had been let down by many people before, this hurt much more than anything else. He wouldn't let her see how much she had hurt him, thought Jatin, as he pulled his defences all the way up. Her lips were moving and he focused on what she was saying.

"What are you doing to yourself, Jatin? Look at yourself. You have become so thin and…"

"Get lost, Aditi! You no longer have a right to tell me how to live my life."

He noted the hurt look on her face with some satisfaction. She had hurt him and he wanted to do the same.

"Who are you punishing, Jatin?" responded Aditi, frustration dripping from her voice. "I know you very well and I know this behaviour. If you are angry with me, then fight with me, but don't do this to yourself."

Jatin pushed her away.

"What do you want from me? Tell me why are you here? To offer me money or to invite me to your wedding?"

She was silent and Jatin walked past her to sit on the corner of the bed. He felt weak although he did not show it. She followed him and knelt down before him.

"Jatin, did you read my letters?" she asked and followed the involuntary movement of his eyes to see the unopened pile of letters which stood at a corner of his study table. She sighed out loud.

"So, you haven't! I had thought so. Please listen to me, Jatin. I came here because I need your help. I wrote so many letters to you, but you didn't reply to a single one, so I had no choice but to come here to meet you. I need your help, Jatin…"

The anguish that Jatin felt made him miss the note of desperation in her voice and he replied harshly.

"Go away, Aditi. We have nothing to do with each other anymore and I would prefer to keep it that way. You cannot throw me out of your life when you wish and then come back again when it suits you. Please leave."

"Jatin, please," she said, her voice breaking. "I know you are hurt, but please give me a chance to explain myself. I was going to the station to leave with you like we had planned that day, but Baba caught me. I had the money and some jewellery with me and he threatened me that if I left home, then he would get you arrested on charges of stealing money and kidnapping and I was scared for you. Baba is a judge. He is a powerful man. Not only can he throw you in jail, but he can, and would have, destroyed Meshomashai's career in law as well—"

Jatin waved a dismissive hand towards her. The only thing that he could think about was that Sandip was waiting outside his door for Aditi. She had betrayed his lifetime of trust.

"I don't care about your sob stories, Aditi. I am no longer as naive as I used to be. I know you and the likes of you very well. I had been blind all along, but now I see everything clearly. I must thank you for opening my eyes. I can now see that I was only a toy for you to play with all through your childhood. Something for you to use and then throw away when you've had your fill. And you know what? I would have understood even that, but do you know what disgusts me the most about you? It's your hypocrisy; your pretence of being a saint."

He watched the tears leak out of the corners of her eyes and felt a strange mix of vindication and guilt at once.

"Shut up, Jatin and stop being so mean. I came all the way from Burdwan to Calcutta, without informing anyone at home, because I need your help. But you won't even listen to me."

"Well, darling, in that case, you've come to the wrong man. Let me remind you in case you have forgotten, Sandip Gupta is your fiancé now and the man is waiting for you outside. I can see that you now have him wrapped around your finger the way you had me earlier. How do you do it? He is the man whom you are looking for, unless…"

Jatin leaned in towards her, "Unless, you've come here under the garb of excuses and sob stories to get laid, like how you used to back in Burdwan. If you want it so bad that you've come all the way here from Burdwan, then I won't turn you away. Come on baby, let's do it!"

For the next few minutes, Jatin acted like a man possessed. He grabbed her and pushed her down on the bed, lying down on top of her. He flung her dupatta away, slipped his hands under her kurta and ran them all over her body, lowered his mouth onto her lips, biting down hard on them until he could taste her blood in his mouth. He did not hear her pleas for him to stop until she slapped him hard across the face and pushed him away from her.

"Stop it, Jatin!" she shouted as she sat up between sobs, putting her dupatta back around her shoulders. "You are disgusting. All my life, I have done everything that I could to try and make you happy, and you have gladly taken everything that I had to offer… right from my kindness to my body. I fed you with the food from the table in our house when you did not have enough to eat and I took care of you when you lay sick and alone in bed, with no money for medicines and no one to look after you. But you seem to have forgotten all of that, and now, when I need your help, you will not even listen to me. My father is right about you. You are just a selfish low-life, Jatin. People like you are scum, who only know how to take and I am sorry that I ever came here!"

Her words caused the childhood wounds to be ripped open. Jatin had not realised that it could hurt so much.

"Get lost, Aditi!" he said. "I hope that I never see you again."

"You won't! That's my promise to you," she said.

He watched her get up and walk out of the house, slamming the door on her way out.

Fifteen

Ten days had passed since Aditi had visited Jatin. During this time, he went through a whole gamut of emotions, which came and went in waves. At first, the pain returned. It was the same feeling that he had felt when he had been thrown out of Aditi's house in Burdwan. A pain at being let down by someone whom he had deeply trusted and depended upon. This was then replaced by anger, which was directed at Aditi, at his father, at Sandip, and above all, at himself. And finally came defiance when Jatin told himself to forget everything that had happened and to move on. If Aditi could forget him so easily, then so could he. He deserved a chance at happiness too, he told himself.

He decided to cut all ties with Burdwan and everyone from there, and start life anew. The letters that Aditi had written to him still sat unopened on his desk. He collected those letters as well as all the unsent letters that he had written to her and burnt them in the sink in his kitchen. Black fumes rose from them and filled his lungs, causing him to choke. Yet the action did nothing to reduce the heaviness in his heart. He sank down to his knees on the kitchen floor, doubling over to place his head between his knees. He tried to think of a reason to continue living. For a moment, he could think of none. And then the images of the National Medical College campus, Shyam gasping for his life, and the possibility of another chance to be a doctor came to his mind. Jatin clutched on to the thin ray of hope desperately.

It was eleven o'clock on a Monday morning when Jatin walked through the crowded campus of the National Medical College and reached the Dean's office. The office was a large room with a high ceiling, big windows which had vertical bars across them and bookshelf-lined walls. Jatin felt intimidated as he entered the office and greeted the dean, Dr Banerjee. He was a lean man, with a head full of salt and pepper hair and a full beard. He sat behind a wooden table that was cluttered with books and papers and studied Jatin who stood nervously before him.

"Take a seat, Jatin," he said motioning towards a chair.

Jatin did as he was told and breathed deeply, trying to control the rapid beating of his heart.

"Relax!" said Dr Banerjee, observing him through sharp eyes. "Here. Let me see your file."

Jatin placed the file that he was carrying with him in the dean's outstretched hand and looked at the man anxiously while he leafed through it. Several minutes passed in silence with the only sound in the room being the loud ticking of the huge clock.

Its sound grated on Jatin's already frazzled nerves and made him even more nervous. Finally Dr Banerjee looked up at him through small but intelligent-looking eyes.

"You have good grades, Jatin," he began. "However, I can see that you have been expelled from your previous college based on some serious allegations against you. Let me see what it says here."

The man re-adjusted the glasses on the bridge of his nose and read verbatim from the file.

"Breaking into a faculty member's house, getting arrested and resorting to violence within the college premises."

The Dean placed the folder back on the table and fixed Jatin with a thoughtful gaze.

"That's quite a long and serious list of offences, Jatin. Would you care to explain?"

Jatin swallowed to clear his throat. This was how all the conversations had begun in the other colleges in the city where he had gone seeking an admission. This was his last chance. He knew that the only thing he could do now was to tell the dean the complete truth, and hope that he would believe him.

"Sir, I belong to a small town called Burdwan situated about a hundred kilometres away from Calcutta. I came to this city to study medicine," began Jatin. "I have always had good grades, as you can see from my certificates. Based on those, I got admission to one of the best medical colleges in the country, along with a national scholarship to fund my education. I came prepared to study hard and I was also doing well in my courses, but sir, I was not prepared for many other things…"

He stopped and looked at the Dean, searching for the familiar condescension and disbelief, but he found none. Instead, the man nodded towards him to continue.

"A group of senior boys at the college used to rag me and most other first year boys," Jatin continued. "They used to beat me, humiliate me, make me parade naked before them, force me to smoke and drink and would even take away my monthly stipend."

Although Jatin had prepared this speech for hours before the bathroom mirror, but reliving those memories made streams of perspiration run down the side of his face. He paused to get a grip on his emotions, wondering whether he had already blown his only chance. Mr Banerjee watched him in silence, pushing a glass of water towards him.

"Drink some water, Jatin," he said gently and the boy gratefully gulped down the water.

"I am very sorry, sir," he began again after regaining his composure and was relieved when Dr Banerjee held up his palm, dismissing the apology. After a few more moments of silence, the Dean spoke, his voice incredulous.

"What I cannot understand is why you did not complain about all of this to the college authorities. From what you tell me, the senior boys were most evidently breaching college protocols and it was well within your rights to raise it to the authorities."

"I was warned by the seniors against this, sir," replied Jatin truthfully. "They were powerful boys and no one usually complained about them. The bully's father was a college trustee too."

The Dean looked unconvinced, but said nothing.

"Alright. Go on," he said.

"I did everything that they told me to do until one day, after the first term exams, they told me to enter one of the professors' house and bring them their answer sheets. I tried to protest but they forced me to go and the professor returned home while I was in his house. He called the police and got me arrested. No one listened to me when I tried to explain my situation and the seniors had disappeared. I had to stay in a police lock-up overnight and when I was out the next morning sir, I could not think straight anymore."

"So, you went to the college and beat up those boys in full view of everyone?" finished Dr Banerjee for him.

Jatin looked at the man, who surprisingly had a tinge of a smile around his mouth.

"Sir, I made a mistake," continued Jatin. "In fact, I made several mistakes which led to my expulsion and I take responsibility for my actions. I can assure you, sir, that I will make sure that such things do not happen again. All I need is one opportunity. After being expelled, I approached several colleges for an admission, but no one would consider my application so I returned home to Burdwan. I finally got admitted into a law degree at Calcutta University."

"Law?" said the dean looking surprised. "Where did that come from?"

"My father is a lawyer, sir, and he used his connections to arrange for the college to admit me in the middle of the academic year. But sir, I don't want to study law. I want to be a doctor and all I need is one opportunity to correct my earlier mistakes. You can take a look at my grades and it will tell you why the government had offered me a national scholarship," said Jatin, causing the Dean to suppress another smile.

"Dr Banerjee, my reason for wanting to be a doctor is a personal one—" Jatin paused mid-sentence. He had not intended to speak about this, but since he had started the sentence, he knew that he would have to complete it.

"I lost my mother when I was very young and she had died due to the lack of proper medical attention. Since then, I had decided that I would be a doctor and would ensure that no one would have to die like that again."

He stopped abruptly, not knowing what more to say. There were a few moments of silence in the room after this touching admission and then the Dean cleared his throat.

"This is a ruthless world and medicine is a ruthless profession, Jatin, as you have already experienced. Do you think that you will be able to hold on to your idealism?"

Jatin had no reply. He kept his head bowed and Dr Banerjee continued.

"Thank you for sharing your story with me. I understand that it is hard for you to speak about all that has happened and I truly feel that our profession would do well to have passionate young people like you in it. I have also heard about your bravery and presence of mind the other night from my young colleagues Amit and Anand. But you must understand that this is a decision that I cannot take unilaterally. I will speak with my colleagues to see if we can offer you an admission. Give me some time and the office will be in touch with you once we have reached a decision on your application."

Jatin walked out of the main building of the college which housed the Dean's office and started to make his way towards the gate. It was the middle of the day and the college was bustling with life. Groups of students hung around outside the college canteen, while others dashed around in an attempt to reach their designated classes on time. The ray of hope that Jatin had received after speaking with Dr Banerjee was the first piece of good news that he had got in a long time. It was enough to make him feel lighter. He wished that he could share this news with someone, but realised that he had no one left in his life with whom he could share his happiness.

Jatin had almost reached the college gates when he heard someone call out his name. He turned around to see a figure clad in a white coat and a standard stethoscope hanging around his neck, rushing towards him among the throng of boys and girls. Jatin hid his face and quickened his pace as he recognised Sandip Gupta. He remembered Aditi telling him that Sandip was an intern at the National Medical College and at present, he was the last person that Jatin wanted to speak with. However, despite Jatin's efforts, Sandip soon caught up with him.

"Hey Jatin. Why are you running away from me?" he said placing an arm around his shoulder which Jatin resisted the urge to flick away.

"Oh! Hi Sandip," he replied awkwardly, avoiding eye-contact.

Sandip had always been good-looking and during their time in school, he had been the resident heart-throb among women. Jatin noted grudgingly that it was still the case as several female students who passed them by, cast admiring glances in Sandip's direction.

"I am in a bit of a hurry today, Sandip," said Jatin, in an attempt to shake him off. "Perhaps we can speak some time later."

"Come on, Jatin! Come and have a cup of tea with me at the canteen," urged Sandip. "We hardly had a chance to speak when we met at your house a few days ago."

"I have to leave, Sandip," said Jatin, hastily pushing past Sandip.

"Hey Jatin!" Sandip called out from behind him, sounding exasperated. "At least let me know when we can meet, now that we are living in the same city. It will be nice to catch up with my favourite junior from school."

Jatin paused. He could feel his temper shoot up. He could not imagine how Sandip could behave as though nothing had happened. Despite the warning bells in his head, Jatin turned and walked back towards Sandip.

"On second thoughts, let's go to the canteen and have some tea, Sandip," he said. "You are getting married to Aditi and that certainly calls for a celebration!"

Sandip looked taken aback. Jatin noted with satisfaction that he seemed to be at a loss of words for a few moments.

"What are you saying, Jatin? Didn't Aditi tell you when she came to meet you the other day?"

"Tell me what, Sandip? What is left to say? All of you are exactly the same and you guys disgust me," said Jatin, unleashing his pent up anger on Sandip.

"But Jatin, Aditi and I are not getting married. I thought that you already knew that."

Jatin looked at Sandip, his mouth hanging open.

"What? But Aditi had told me that…"

"Yes. Our parents wanted us to get married, but Aditi refused. She had many arguments with her parents and her father made her promise to never meet with you again. He had threatened to get you thrown in jail using his influence and Aditi was so scared that she agreed to not meet with you. But in return, she made a bargain with him that she would never get married to anyone else."

Jatin staggered backwards. He saw clearly how he had misunderstood Aditi all along. He remembered how he had turned her away when she had come to see him in Calcutta. Looking back, he could understand the pain reflected on her face as she left his house.

"But Sandip," he said, "Do you know why Aditi had come to see me? And why did you accompany her? I thought you two were engaged."

Sandip gave him a surprised look.

"I have no idea why she wanted to see you, Jatin. I assumed that you must have spoken to each other since you spent so much time together that day. Aditi had written to me a few days ago, saying that she needed to come to Calcutta to meet you urgently, and she needed my help since she had never travelled alone. No one in her family knew that she had come here to see you. I went to Burdwan and brought her over to the address of your house that she had given me. After leaving your house that day, she seemed very upset, although she didn't tell me anything. I dropped her back to her house in Burdwan. I know nothing other than this."

Sandip must have noted the stricken look on Jatin's face.

"Jatin," he said, "in case you haven't spoken with Aditi, then I would recommend that you do that as soon as you can. She was very worried and seemed to need help. Please talk to her and see if you can help her."

Moments later, Jatin walked out of the college premises and headed home, along the now familiar Calcutta streets which were relatively empty during the middle of the day. There were only a few fellow pedestrians along with him on the sidewalk and an occasional empty bus rushed past on the street beside. Lost in his thoughts, Jatin did not realise that he had stepped off the sidewalk and was walking down the middle of the road, until he heard the bell of a hand-pulled rickshaw behind him.

"Watch where you are walking, brother!" cried the rickshaw puller as he passed Jatin by, carrying two passengers in his carriage.

He jumped back on the sidewalk and continued walking. He recalled Aditi's visit to his house a few weeks ago. Now, with his mind clearer than it had been at that time, he could see that she had desperately wanted to tell him something, but he had been so hurt that he hadn't allowed her to speak. She surely must have had something important to say, thought Jatin. Something that mattered enough to make her travel from Burdwan to Calcutta. He felt like kicking himself, wishing that he had been patient enough to listen to her before brutally insulting her and turning her away.

As Jatin turned into Ballygunge, he decided to call Aditi, from Mr Ganguly's house upstairs, as soon as he reached home. He knew that she would be hurt and angry with him, but he told himself that he would apologise to her and then everything would be alright again. By the time he reached the gates of the house, Jatin was running and almost bumped in to Mr Ganguly, who was standing near the gate.

"Jatin, I have been waiting for you," said the man and Jatin looked at the short, pot-bellied man in surprise. In all the time that he had spent in the house, he had never known his landlord to wait for him to return home, except on occasions when the weekly rent had been due. This time, though, he remembered having paid the rent only a few days ago.

"Your father had called about an hour ago and he wants you to leave for Burdwan as soon as you can," said Mr Ganguly.

Jatin stared at the man, focusing on his two protruding front teeth. His father had not communicated with him since he had left home.

"W-what happened?" he asked the man, not knowing what to expect.

Mr Ganguly paused for a while and said, " Jatin, I am afraid that there is some bad news that I will have to convey to you."

His words made Jatin's heart go cold in anticipation.

"Your father told me that your friend, Aditi, is unwell. He wanted you to go back to Burdwan as soon as you can. I suggest that you take the afternoon train out of Calcutta, Jatin. That way, you will reach Burdwan before dark."

The loud clanging of a tram passing by the house arrested Jatin's attention. It was the first time that he had looked closely at the omnipresent vehicle during his stay in the city. He found himself staring at a painting on the outside wall of the tram which showed the smiling face of a woman who was holding out a packet of Saridon towards him. Jatin wondered if the medicine was really as effective as they claimed on the radio and on the various hoardings around the city. He would have to try it out someday, he thought.

Sixteen

The first thing that Jatin noticed was how pale her face looked. It was almost as though someone had drawn all the blood out of her body, leaving the veins that lay beneath her smooth skin looking transparent and empty. Her usually wheatish skin was as white as the sheets on the bed on which she lay. Her wild, curly locks were spread out on the pillow, making a halo around her small face. He took a step inside the bedroom which he had visited hundreds of times before and looked around to notice that everything looked exactly like how he remembered it.

The blue and white dressing table stood next to the window near the far corner of the room; a wooden desk and chair with books neatly arranged on it was situated next to the dressing table; a cupboard stood beside the desk, on the door of which was pasted a life-size black-and-white picture of Dev Anand, Aditi's favourite movie star. Jatin remembered that the poster had been a topic of several debates in the Sanyal household, but it had still managed to withstand the ravages of time and parental disapproval, thus sealing its place on the cupboard door. The only other piece of furniture in the room was the four poster bed, where Aditi now lay. Jatin stood next to the bed, looking down at her. To his eyes, except for the paleness, she looked fine. He was sure that she would wake up as soon as she knew that he was back in town. There was so much that he wanted to tell her and so much more left to do together.

"Aditi?"

He gently shook her by the shoulder, trying to get her to open her eyes, but she did not budge. Jatin frowned. He touched her forehead to brush away the few errant strands of hair that had fallen over it and recoiled as he felt the coldness of her skin.

How could everyone be so careless? She was cold and he would have to find her a shawl to cover her with. The red one that she usually wore must be around somewhere.

He began to frantically look around the room for the shawl. He looked under the covers at the foot of the bed and threw open the doors of the cupboard to rummage through the neatly-arranged clothes in it. Annoyingly, his vision was blurred which made it difficult for him to see properly, and he repeatedly rubbed his eyes with the back of his palm

"Jatin... *Jatin...*"

He looked up irritably to find himself face to face with his step-mother. He was mildly surprised since he didn't remember seeing her when he had entered the room, and it had seemed that he and Aditi were alone in there. Mrs Majumdar was crying and he wondered why. He cast the thought aside as he did not have time to think about that. Perhaps he would ask her later about it. Later, once he had found the shawl and covered Aditi with it.

"Jatin, what are you looking for?" asked Mrs Majumdar, trying to restrain his frantic movements.

"A shawl… Aditi's shawl. Have you seen it? She is cold."

"Jatin... please. Stop!"

But Jatin could not stop. For the moment, his entire existence seemed to depend on finding that shawl. He had a feeling that something terrible would happen if he did not find it.

"Please, leave me alone," he said, pushing her away. "Let me get the shawl from downstairs. Aditi must have left it there. She is so careless."

He started towards the door of the room when someone caught him by the upper arm and turned him around. Jatin spun around feeling desperate and lashed out to push the person out of his way. Before he could react, he felt the crack of a sharp slap on his cheek. The impact made him break out of the trance that he was in and as his vision cleared, he found himself before Aditi's mother. She caught him by the cuff of the woollen sweater that he was wearing and shook him hard while he stood frozen. He stared at the woman before him, who was no more the soft-spoken mother of his friend that he had known for most of his life. He could see that she was upset and presuming it to be about her daughter, he wanted to tell her that Aditi was alright, but found the words frozen in his throat. She slapped him hard, again.

"Why are you here? Why have you come back? What do you want from us now?"

He said nothing. Neither did he resist her attacks. He continued to look at her silently, wondering how similar Aditi and her mother looked. Mrs Sanyal had the same curly locks as her daughter, although her hair was now interspersed with grey. She had the same bright eyes which were now swollen from crying and the same wheatish complexion which was now botched with red patches as a mixture of tears and snot flowed down her face.

"You've killed my daughter Jatin. You've killed my Aditi!"

Her words sent a sharp pain shooting through him, which hurt in the remotest parts of his body, that he hadn't even known existed.

"Get out of my house!" screamed Aditi's mother, shaking him as hard as she could. "I don't want to see you… ever again."

A few women clad in white sarees, who had been unnoticed by Jatin so far, emerged from the shadows near the corners of the room and grabbed Mrs Sanyal's arms, pulling her away from him. He watched on as the women led her outside the room. He ran his eyes around him, surprised to find that the room was full of people, all of whose accusatory glances rested on him, seemingly unified in their verdict of his crime.

"Jatin…"

He felt a pat on his shoulder. His father seemed to have aged ten years since the last time that he had seen the man less than two months ago.

"Baba?" he croaked as the constriction in his throat cleared, allowing words to flow out

"Thank god you are here, son. I was worried that you would be late."

"Late for what?" he asked, trying to push away the horrible reality that was beginning to settle in, despite the protests of his mind. As he spoke, he could hear his voice echo hollowly in his ears.

His father studied him for a moment and then placed his arm around Jatin's shoulders.

"Jatin," he said softly. "Come outside. I need to speak with you."

He continued to tell himself that this was a nightmare and as soon as he woke up, everything would be alright again. He allowed himself to be led out of the room, down the staircase and into the garden walkway outside the house. He looked up and noticed that the sky was overcast with dark clouds, although it was the middle of winter.

"Jatin," said his father, drawing back his attention towards him. "Aditi's gone…"

"Gone?" he said irritably. "What do you mean that she has gone? She is inside, sleeping, and I need to speak with her, but no one will allow me to do that. It's very important for me to talk to her…"

He was rambling; his words falling over each other and coming out incoherently. But now that his voice was back, Jatin could not stop talking. It was important for him to hear the sound of his voice in his head, so that it could replace the horrible thoughts that were forming in his mind.

"Jatin," his father's stern voice cut through his words, "Look at me."

He disobeyed. He continued to mumble while he looked down at his shoes, at the gravel that was beneath his feet and at the few shreds of grass that escaped through the gravel and managed to surface for fresh air. As he continued to ramble, Jatin could feel his breath come in short sharp gasps and he could feel the damn constriction return to his throat.

"Jatin… shut up and look at me!"

His father's voice was sharp and Jatin obeyed this time.

"Aditi died this morning. She is gone."

Although Mr Majumdar had spoken the sentence quietly, there was finality in the statement which cut through the fog in Jatin's mind. The reality that was at the fringes of his consciousness finally sank in and he felt a block of cold, heavy lead settle in his heart

"Jatin... there's something more that you need to know."

There was a strange buzzing sound in his ears which was making it difficult for Jatin to hear his father clearly. He leaned forward a little, trying to pay attention.

"Did you know that Aditi was pregnant with what I assume was your child?"

His mind snapped to attention like an elastic band as he looked sharply at his father.

"Answer the question."

He turned his head from side-to-side, noticing that the action took a lot of effort, as though his head was heavily laden with bricks. He missed the look on Mr Majumdar's face who, for a moment, yearned to pull his hurting son in his arms and console him like he used to do when Jatin had been a baby. He had loved that small child, but as the years had passed by, a distance had begun to creep in between them. Now Mr Majumdar knew that the chasm between him and his son had become too wide to bridge.

He continued to speak, "I am surprised that she said nothing to anyone about it, and believed that she could handle everything on her own. I had thought that she would have shared the news with you at least."

Several questions that had been in Jatin's mind for weeks were now answered at once. Now he knew why Aditi had come to see him in Calcutta. He could now see the reason for the desperation in her eyes when he had turned her away. And he could now feel her pain when he had said what were to be his final words to her – *Get lost, Aditi. I hope that I never see you again.*

He returned his attention to what Mr Majumdar was saying.

"The doctor who came to see her this morning told us that she was about three months pregnant. She must have been scared to tell anyone about it, but I still wish that she had talked to someone. Instead, she decided to try to abort the child on her own."

The block of lead grew heavier as he gaped at his father. He was still having trouble hearing him.

"There's no way to tell the exact time, but sometime last night, she used a knitting needle to attempt an abortion, and it damaged some organs, leading to an internal hemorrhage. She lost a lot of blood. The doctor mentioned that she could have survived, if only she had called someone last night. But she didn't, or perhaps she did, and no one heard her. We will never know the answer. And when her mother went to wake her up today morning, by then it was already too late.

"No!" it was a scream. *"No!"*

Jatin could feel the constriction in his throat explode, and course through his whole body like a wet, slimy fluid. His legs gave way and he sank to the ground. His palms and knees pressed down on the rough, wet gravel. His mind was blank and he suddenly felt very cold, beginning to shiver as he became aware of the cold unseasonal rain that lashed his body.

Aditi's mother had been right. He was responsible for the death of the woman whom he loved... and also of his unborn child.

"Jatin," his father was kneeling by his side, "Get up and go inside! See her one more time before they take her away for the cremation."

The word cremation reached his ears clearly, managing to cut through the constant buzzing sound in his ears. He stared at his father for a moment, who nodded towards the house. He felt a rush of adrenaline course through his body, causing him to dash inside the house and run up the stairs, two at a time, until he reached Aditi's bedside. He paused to steady his heavy breathing. He felt an unprecedented sense of calmness come over him as he knelt by her side and took her hand in his, noticing how cold it felt. He watched her familiar face which looked unperturbed by everything around her and leaned forward to speak with her.

"Aditi, when I boarded the train to come to Burdwan, I had so many things that I wanted to tell you… things that we had dreamed of together. I knew they would make you very happy. But now, none of that has any value anymore. Now I only want to say that I am sorry. I am sorry for not being there with you when you needed me the most; for turning you away when you had come to me looking for help; and for being so caught up with my own small problems that I failed to see your bigger ones. I have no excuses to make and, for this, I will never be able to forgive myself for as long as I live."

He stroked her hair, feeling its characteristic softness beneath his fingers for the last time.

"Only you understood why I wanted to be a doctor. It was because I wanted to heal people and save lives, so that no one would have to die in the way that my mother did. But in that quest, I could not save the life that was most precious to me."

He could hear sniffles coming from the shadows around the room, however his own eyes were dry and his voice was steady.

"I am sorry that you had to bear, what must have seemed like a burden, of our unborn child all by yourself. And I am sorry that I wasn't by your side during those last few minutes when I know you must have been scared. I know well how scared you are of blood. But all that is over now dear, and I hope that you are happy and free of all the pain."

He stopped abruptly and stood up, with his body stiff as though it would crack if he so much as moved an additional muscle.

"Goodbye, Aditi," he said softly, taking a last look at her face and then turned and walked out of the room.

Although it wasn't too late in the evening, darkness had descended over their small town. The light drizzle from earlier in the day had now intensified as the skies opened up and heavy rain flooded the streets. Jatin walked towards the gate of Aditi's house, his head hung. He knew that this was the last time that he would ever come here. Before leaving, he turned around one last time to look at the now empty window of her bedroom, where he had been so accustomed to seeing her face. He had always taken her presence in his life for granted, assuming that she would be there, waiting for him whenever he cared to turn around to look for her. In his mad pursuit of material happiness, he had pushed away the rare gift of unconditional love that she had offered him. He looked at the empty road that stretched out in front of him and felt a sudden urge to run. He wanted to run as fast as he could so that he could outrun the pain and get rid of the vacuum that had been formed inside him.

He discovered that his vision was blurred again and angrily rubbed at his eyes with the back of his hand, unaware of the tears that ran down his face. A car came up in front of him and screeched to a halt, barely avoiding hitting him. Jatin stumbled over the stationary car and looked through the glass at the angry driver inside. The man was saying something to him, but he could not hear him and had no time to stop. He continued to run, not knowing where he was headed. He passed by their house, which was next to Aditi's, and remembered her visits to him every morning for as long as he had lived in Burdwan. He turned a corner and entered the next lane where their old, single-room house was situated and memories surfaced – of her bringing him food every afternoon, at a time when he used to be scared and hungry. Jatin quickened his pace so that he could leave the horrible house behind and passed by the park, which had been their favourite spot, where they had spent many lazy afternoons together. He ran faster and faster so that he could outrun the memories, and soon could see the railway station in the distance. He remembered waiting there for Aditi on a cold, windy morning, not too long ago, when they had planned to go away and live their lives together.

All of that seemed so far back in the past now and all their well-laid plans had been shattered to pieces. He ran past the station and followed the railway track, leaving the town far behind. But no matter how far he ran, the vacuum within him continued to grow until he was unable to breathe anymore. He opened his mouth and let out short gasps, attempting to fill his lungs with air; finally collapsing in a heap by the side of the tracks. He made a futile attempt to raise himself and continue running, but he was drained of energy and welcomed the darkness that appeared before his eyes.

Epilogue

Present Day
Burdwan, Jatin's house

He stirred in his sleep and cracked open his eyes. He was lying on his bed at eighty-one years of age. The clock on the bedside stand showed twelve o'clock. The drapes over the windows were still open and the stars twinkled at him from above. He realised that he had been dreaming about Aditi yet again, and as always, she seemed so real in his sleep, as though she were right next to him. His eyes swept the room, looking for her. And for a moment he panicked, as he stared into the darkness of the room, trying to find her. He was sure that she was hidden somewhere in the shadows where he couldn't see her yet. She had always been mischievous. She had always enjoyed teasing him. Jatin sat up slowly in bed and called out to her.

"Aditi? Are you there?"

He detected a slight movement near the corner of the room and Aditi's petite figure emerged as the moonlight from the window outside illuminated her. The soft curls fell around her face; the cotton salwar kameez was loosely draped around her body and she had a playful twinkle in her eyes.

Dear Aditi! Always eighteen; never nineteen.

She had started visiting him again, about a year ago, and initially Jatin had been resistant to her appearances. During the first few instances, he would pretend not to see her when she would appear, seemingly out of nowhere, at his bedside during the early hours of the morning. Or he would find her hovering outside the front door whenever he opened it. But as time passed, Jatin got accustomed to her visits and even found himself looking forward to seeing her; worrying when he didn't see her for a day or two. Lately, the frequency of her visits had increased and Jatin had even started talking with her, which, he discovered, came easily to him, although decades had passed in the interim. She would appear at his doorstep at various times during the day, just like in the old days with the same request on her lips.

"Come on, Jatin! Let's go out."

He resisted that urge and would firmly shake his head and shut the door on her disappointed face.

Now as he looked at the girl before him, Jatin patted the bed beside him, beckoning her to join him. She obliged, jumping on to the high bed which left her feet swinging a few inches above the floor. Jatin looked at her affectionately. He realised that he had never apologised to her for all that he had done and yet she had found it in her kind heart to forgive him.

"Aditi?"

She looked at his wizened face. The young, ambitious boy that she had been madly in love with was long gone. What remained now was a tired, lonely man.

"I have never apologised to you before. I never had the opportunity to do so, but I am sorry for everything. I was young and arrogant. Back in those days, I only thought about myself and could see nothing else; not even you..."

He trailed off and they sat in silence for a few moments.

"After you, I never could love anyone again," Jatin spoke again. "I never got married, but..." he turned towards her, "... but, I did finally become a doctor. I managed to get admission to the National Medical College in Calcutta. After completing my education, I returned to Burdwan, the place that I had always wanted to run away from. I realised that I owed a lot to my town and to the people here. You know how bad the medical conditions used to be here in those days. I realised that if we had any good doctors in town back then, then perhaps Ma and you would have stayed longer. I wanted to try and change that, so I came back here and set up my medicine practice. Since then I have worked to heal as many people as I could, but..."

"Jatin," she said softly, cutting into his words. "If you still love me, then will you do something for me?"

"Anything," he replied, "anything!"

She stood up and stretched her arm out to him.

"Then come with me, Jatin. Let's go out."

She was standing before him with her hand outstretched.

Jatin locked his eyes with hers, and at that instant, he knew that he had been waiting for this moment for his whole life. The interim years that he had spent after losing Aditi had meant very little to him and he realised that all that time had been spent in preparation for this moment today. Once more, Jatin found himself faced with making the same decision that he had been faced with this very girl… years ago. He had made a blunder then – a mistake – that had changed both his life as well as the lives of several others, forever.

Today, he finally had the opportunity to correct the blunder that he had made as an immature teenager. He took a deep breath and raised his hand to reach Aditi's outstretched one. He noticed that the tremors in his hand were back and he fought to keep it still. She reached forward and grasped his hand in her steady one.

And all at once, Jatin felt the years fall away. He jumped up from the bed, not feeling the pain in his creaking bones anymore and followed Aditi out of the room. The moon that had been a loyal witness to his life through the years now shone on the eighty-one-year-old lifeless body that lay behind on the crumpled bed.

Recommended Reading

LOVE BEYOND THE HORIZON

Madhu Vajpayee

Dr Avni is trying to start her life afresh after a bitter past when she meets Dr Aakash. Behind the strict senior doctor is a man trying to find a reason to go on in life. Destiny brings them together, but will they be able to beat all odds to stay in love?

ISBN: 978-9390441211; Pages: 216; Format: Paperback; Price: INR 250

BROKEN BY LOVE

Shalaka Nadhe

Sushmita and Sumit complement each other perfectly. When business tycoon Raghav falls in love with Sushmita, there is chaos in their lives. Read to know what happens when love becomes an obsession.

ISBN: 978-9390441129; Pages: 168; Format: Paperback; Price: INR 199

THE LOVER IN MY DREAMS

Shivani Singhal

Naina is a modern girl stuck within the confines of a conservative family. She is on the verge of falling in love when her match is fixed with someone else by her parents. Caught between her mind and heart, she stumbles upon secrets from her past that she could never have imagined.

ISBN: 978-9390441143; Pages: 216; Format: Paperback; Price: INR 250

THE PROMISES WE MADE

Rohan Jain

Raj is thrilled to be going to Switzerland for his internship. Meeting Sofia there feels like a dream coming true, bringing to life his most fond wishes. Until destiny plays its cruel card, throwing Raj and his heart into a turmoil of love, loss and pain.

ISBN: 978-9390441051; Pages: 208; Format: Paperback; Price: INR 225

www.ingramcontent.com/pod-product-compliance
Ingram Content Group UK Ltd.
Pitfield, Milton Keynes, MK11 3LW, UK
UKHW040004200726
13854UKWH00001B/28

9 789390 441235